DATE DUE

GAYLORD   PRINTED IN U.S.A.

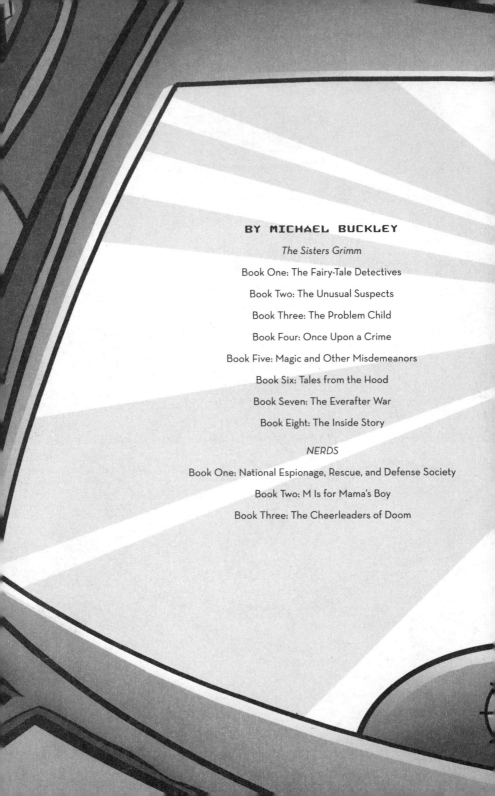

BY MICHAEL BUCKLEY

The Sisters Grimm

Book One: The Fairy-Tale Detectives

Book Two: The Unusual Suspects

Book Three: The Problem Child

Book Four: Once Upon a Crime

Book Five: Magic and Other Misdemeanors

Book Six: Tales from the Hood

Book Seven: The Everafter War

Book Eight: The Inside Story

NERDS

Book One: National Espionage, Rescue, and Defense Society

Book Two: M Is for Mama's Boy

Book Three: The Cheerleaders of Doom

NERDS

THE CHEERLEADERS OF DOOM
• BOOK THREE •

MICHAEL BUCKLEY

Illustrations by
ETHEN BEAVERS

AMULET BOOKS

NEW YORK

HM 0215
JF
9-2011
$14.95

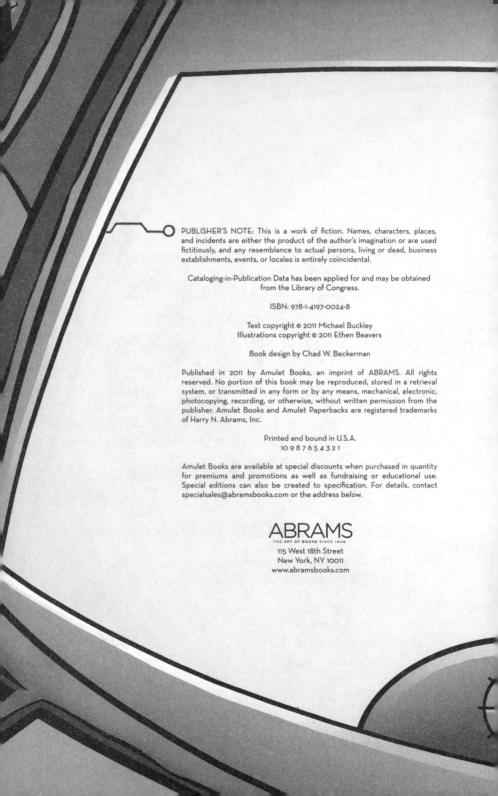

Cataloging-in-Publication Data has been applied for and may be obtained from the Library of Congress.

ISBN: 978-1-4197-0024-8

Text copyright © 2011 Michael Buckley
Illustrations copyright © 2011 Ethen Beavers

Book design by Chad W. Beckerman

Printed and bound in U.S.A.
10 9 8 7 6 5 4 3 2 1

Amulet Books are available at special discounts when purchased in quantity for premiums and promotions as well as fundraising or educational use. Special editions can also be created to specification. For details, contact specialsales@abramsbooks.com or the address below.

ABRAMS
THE ART OF BOOKS SINCE 1949

115 West 18th Street
New York, NY 10011
www.abramsbooks.com

For Abigail Contessa
and her very cool
mom, Molly Choi

Prologue

Twelve-year-old Gerdie Baker frowned at her reflection in her bedroom mirror. She had long and lumpy limbs; huge, Hobbit-like feet; hair like a tumbleweed in an old cowboy movie; and an unfortunate under-bite that made her look like a caveman. She was a mess, which led her to one undeniable conclusion: She must be a Bigfoot. Like Bigfoots, she lumbered when she walked. Like Bigfoots, she scared small animals. Like Bigfoots, she grunted when she ate.

Since her parents weren't Bigfoots, she concluded that she must have been discovered in the wilds and transplanted to the suburbs of Akron, Ohio, for study. It was the only reasonable explanation.

To prove her theory she had done a few simple calculations:

- There was a 40% chance that her family had found her on a camping trip, shaved her down, and taught her to speak.
- There was a 35% chance that she was part of an experiment by the Department of Fish and Wildlife in hopes of integrating Bigfoots into modern society.
- There was a 23% chance that she had broken free from a cage in a traveling sideshow.
- And then, there was the teeny-tiny 2% chance that she wasn't a missing link at all but a twelve-year-old girl suffering through a very awkward period. This 2% was only on the list because Bigfoots are not known for their math skills, and so the fact that she could construct these possibilities left a hole in her theory.

She was devising a new list of theories on why a Bigfoot might know calculus when she heard a loud squeal coming through her open bedroom window. Gerdie walked over and looked outside into the backyard. There she saw cake, balloons, a deejay, streamers, punch, a karaoke machine, and two dozen pretty girls in cheerleading outfits having the time of their lives. Her birthday party was obnoxious.

Her mother had gone all out this year for Gerdie and her sisters, Linda and Luanne—otherwise known as the Baker Triplets. But Gerdie could not bring herself to go down and join the fun. Just because she shared their DNA (as her mother claimed) didn't mean she was one of them. Linda, Luanne, and their friends were all gorgeous, like they had stepped out of a fashion magazine. "Gruesome Gerdie" looked like she had crawled out of *Field and Stream*. Her mind couldn't help but calculate what would happen if she were to show her face at the party.

- There was a 54% chance that the girls would laugh at her.
- A 29% chance that they would stare at her like she was from another planet.
- A 10% chance that someone would scream and/or faint and/or vomit.
- And a 7% chance that someone would call Animal Control and have her shot with a tranquilizer dart.

Nope. She didn't belong down there . . . yet. But soon, very soon, she would be one of the pretty ones. She, too, would be the center of attention. You see, Gerdie Baker had plans. Which was probably further evidence that she was not really a Bigfoot. Bigfoots don't spend a lot of time thinking about the future. She would have to increase the 2% to 3%.

She sat down on her bed, snatched a notebook off her nightstand, and opened it to a math problem. This one was more complicated than anything she had ever attempted. It stretched out over dozens of pages, x's and y's holding on to pluses and minuses like life preservers in a murky sea. Soon, she would fish them out and unlock their mysteries and her miserable life would change forever. If only she still had her—

There was a knock at the door.

"Leave me alone. I don't want any cake," Gerdie shouted.

But the knock came again.

Setting down her notebook, she crossed the room and threw open the door. There was no one there. She craned her neck into the hallway, but it was empty. She glanced down and saw an envelope on the floor. It was addressed to her. She scooped it up.

Inside was a note that read, *There are presents for you downstairs.*

Gerdie sighed. She might as well go down, get the presents, and get it over with.

In the backyard a sea of surprised girls stared at her. The 29% had been correct. She could almost hear the confusion in their minds as the guests tried to understand how she could be related to Linda and Luanne. Maybe coming downstairs hadn't been a good idea.

"Have some cake, Gertrude," her mother said as she approached with Gerdie's sisters in tow.

Gerdie eyed the birthday cake. It was shaped like a megaphone—the kind cheerleaders use at football games. It read, *Happy Birthday, Luanne, Linda, and G.*

"G?"

Gerdie's mom looked defensive. "Honey, Gertrude is a long name. There's only so much cake! Where are all the friends you invited?"

"She doesn't have any friends to invite." Linda laughed.

"I used to before we moved," Gerdie cried. "I had lots of friends."

"No, you hung around with the nerd herd," Luanne said. "The biggest collection of waste cases in the history of Nathan Hale Elementary. Moving us here was the best thing that could have happened to you."

Gerdie sighed. They had moved from Arlington, Virginia, a year and a half ago, and she had never adjusted. "Well, let's open some presents."

Everyone gathered around a table stacked high with boxes wrapped in pretty bows, and Gerdie's mom handed them out one by one. It took nearly a half hour of unwrapping before she uncovered a present for Gerdie.

Gerdie opened it. It was a dog collar. Linda and Luanne laughed the loudest in a chorus of giggles. Gerdie wanted to throw the collar into the crowd, along with a few well-aimed punches. But her mom quickly handed her another present. "Don't be mad. The girls are just teasing."

Gerdie opened the small box and suddenly her scowl was replaced by a toothy smile. "It's an Inimation 410A!"

"A what?" her mother asked.

"It's a state-of-the-art scientific calculator with over four hundred mathematical functions. It has a two-line display with thirty-two levels of parenthesis! It does formula notation; variable statistics; fraction and decimal conversions; Boolean operations; probability searches; degree, radian, and grad conversions; sine, cosine, and tangent calculations; as well as exponent and trigonometric functions. It also has a hundred and fifty megabytes of memory storage, plus it runs off a solar cell."

Gerdie stopped talking. She knew everyone was staring at her—even the party clown.

"It's very advanced," she finished quietly.

"What a nerd," Luanne said as she, Linda, and her mother left Gerdie to go to the patio, which they were using as a dance floor. Their mom was entirely too old to dance with the girls and their friends, but it didn't stop her from teaching them a goofy dance she called the "Electric Slide." She was giggling like a twelve-year-old.

Gerdie looked around. Who would have bought her such

an amazing present? She shook her head. Oh, who cared! She couldn't wait to test it!

She turned to run back to her room, but standing behind her was a man built like a tree with thick arms and legs. He had jet-black hair with a white stripe down the middle—just like a skunk—and it hung down in his eyes. He had a long, shaggy beard, and an eye as white as snow. At the end of one of his arms was a silver hook where his hand should have been.

"Here's one more," the strange man said, handing Gerdie a thin envelope with his good hand. Just like the envelope upstairs, it was addressed to her. "My employer hopes you have a happy birthday."

"Huh? Who is your employer?" Gerdie asked, but the man turned and hurried away. "Are you with the caterers?"

But he was gone. Gerdie shrugged off the odd encounter and opened the envelope. Inside was a piece of plain white paper that read:

$$X = 41.6443/3$$

"What is it, Gerdie? You look like you don't feel well," her mother said, stepping off the dance floor for a breath of fresh air.

Gerdie didn't answer. Instead, she darted into the house, up the stairs, and back into her bedroom, slamming the door behind her. She snatched her notebook off the bed, then fumbled to open her new calculator with nervous hands. Once it was powered on, she typed in her equation. Then she punched in the mystery number for the value of x and pressed the Equals button. Suddenly, the calculator buzzed and blinked and bounced around in her hand. Its plastic case got so hot that Gerdie dropped it on the floor. There was a POP! and a CRACKLE! And then the screen went black.

"No!!!" she cried, scooping it back up, ignoring the burns to her hands. She punched the buttons, but there was no life left in it. She tossed it aside and buried her face in her pillow. Tears streamed out of her eyes, soaking her cheeks and lips. She needed the answer to her equation! It would change everything.

And then she heard the Inimation 410A hum to life once more. She sat up, wiped her eyes, and looked down at the calculator lying on the floor. On the screen was flashing a number:

17

17

17

Gerdie couldn't believe what she was seeing. The math problem she had labored over for more than a year and a half was solved. The dark ocean had calmed and the numbers had found dry land in the form of the beautiful number 17!

Gerdie raced to her closet and threw open the door. Inside

was a tube of blue-and-gray drafting paper. She unrolled it on her desk and smoothed it out to reveal the plans for a bizarre-looking machine. It had buttons and knobs and two glass tubes rising out of the top. She studied it like it was a masterpiece hanging in an art museum. Then she glanced down at the mysterious letter still crumpled in her hand. Attached to the paper with the equation was another letter, this one on stationery from a place called the Arlington Hospital for the Criminally Insane. It was signed, *Happy birthday from your pal Heathcliff.* Gerdie smiled.

"Thank you, Heathcliff. *This* is the best birthday present ever."

THREE DAYS LATER

Gerdie tightened the final screws on her creation. She stepped back to admire her beautiful invention. Two glass tubes rose from the top like bunny ears, straps hung down like limp arms, and its faceplate had a dozen different dials and parts from old video game consoles. In truth, it was an ungainly misfit, but then again, so was its creator. No matter: The government would pay her a fortune for the machine once they saw what it could do.

She tapped the power button and heard the motors turning. A fuzzy map formed on one of the tiny monitors, and after peering at it for a long moment, she punched some coordinates

into the keyboard on its side. It weighed a ton, but she hefted the device onto her back and reached over to push the record button on a mounted video camera. A good scientist always documented her successes and her failures.

"Well, this is the maiden voyage of my machine. I still don't have a name for it, but I'll worry about that if it works. If all goes according to plan, I will vanish from my bedroom and reappear half a block away in the church parking lot," she said. "If not—I don't know. I've never built a teleportation device before, using my allowance as the budget. I know it's probably dangerous to test this in the house, but I just can't resist!"

She awkwardly turned to look at the movie star photos she had taped to her bedroom walls. "If this thing works, I'm going to use every penny to make myself look like you—hair, makeup, dental work—everything. I'll be an all-new me, and Gruesome Gerdie will be a thing of the past."

She flipped the activation switch. Above her head she could hear the glass cathode tubes warming. She gazed upward just in time to see a powerful charge passing back and forth between them, creating a tiny lightning storm of crackling energy. The electricity formed into a spinning ball of perfect light that grew and grew. Its surface was clear and white, but when Gerdie ran her hand through it, she left streaks where her fingers had glided— like smearing icing on a birthday cake. The circle grew bigger than her whole body, and then it floated down from above until it was directly in front of her face. There was an odd tearing sound, like someone was ripping a huge piece of paper in two, and with shocking force Gerdie was dragged into the energy circle.

A split second later she was freezing and blind. She rubbed her eyes into focus. To her surprise, she was not in her bedroom or in the church parking lot. Instead, she was alone in a frozen wasteland that stretched as far as the horizon. Ice covered everything and snow was coming down in blankets, each tiny crystal like a razor cutting at her exposed skin.

"Where am I?" she said, teeth chattering, to no one in particular. There didn't seem to be a living soul for miles. Had she plugged in the wrong latitude and longitude? Had she assembled the machine incorrectly? Had her equations been incorrect?

No! That wasn't possible. Gerdie took great pride in how thorough she was. No matter how simple the problem, she accounted for every possible solution. Her teachers often complained that she made things intentionally difficult. She had once used a whole ream of paper to prove the answer to 2 + 2! Still, here she was, in a place too cold even for Santa Claus. No, something else was wrong. Heathcliff's number must have altered the machine's basic function.

Shivering, Gerdie pushed the plunger on her machine, but

nothing happened. The battery was dead. Her device had a self-charging fuel source, but it would be ten minutes before it was ready to teleport her again. Unfortunately, she was wearing a pair of linen pants and a short-sleeve shirt. She wouldn't survive that long. Her fingers and toes were already numb.

"Help!" she cried. "Is anyone out there?"

Suddenly, she heard something odd. It sounded like footsteps, but how could she hear someone approaching with the roaring wind all around her? "Hello?"

There was no response, just more heavy footfalls, so Gerdie decided to move toward the sound. The weight of the teleportation device wasn't making it easy to trek through the deep snow, but she struggled forward. She climbed up an icy slope, where she thought she could actually hear the heavy breath of her rescuer. But when she reached the crest, she saw something that just couldn't be possible. It was nearly twelve feet high and covered in thick, curly hair. It smelled of mud, and it had long curving tusks that sliced through the air, pointing right at her. She had seen paintings of such creatures in books, and even a skeleton up close at the Smithsonian Institution in Washington, D.C., but they weren't supposed to exist anymore. Even if she had teleported to the North Pole or Antarctica, or wherever she was, the last woolly mammoths died ten thousand years ago.

The beast seemed as startled by her as she was by it, and it reared back on its hind legs. When it came crashing back down, it roared and stomped its huge feet. Gerdie was sure it would charge and crush her flat. She stepped back, missed her footing, then felt herself plunging downward as her machine dragged her to the bottom of the icy slope. She tried to get to her feet, but the weight of the teleportation machine would not let her stand. She struggled out of its straps, then did her best to pull it behind her. She couldn't abandon it. It was her only way back home.

But the mammoth was charging toward her, its huge head down and its tusks aimed at her heart. She rolled into a ball, and the giant creature ran right over her, missing her entirely. Somehow it managed to miss the machine, too.

She scrambled to her feet, but a blast of cold air hit her hard. She lost her grasp on the machine and fell, rolling like a snowball, end over end, until she stopped at the mouth of a cave. Standing over her were three figures wrapped completely in animal hides. They held spears and grunted angrily at her.

The trio leaped forward with spears in hand, but instead of killing her they ran right past and attacked the mammoth. Their weapons were crude—nothing more than sticks with sharp stone points—but they were thrown with deadly accuracy. One went into the creature's front leg and the second into its head. The third caught the beast in the heart. It wailed in agony, finally falling forward onto the snow. The creature was dead.

As she watched, stunned, Gerdie was lifted to her feet by strong hands. More of the strange warriors had stepped out of the cave and were helping her. They pulled her inside the cave, deep into its darkness.

By the light of flickering torches mounted on the walls, she caught glimpses of cave paintings: hunters fighting herds of mammoths, strange deerlike creatures, something she thought might have been a saber-toothed tiger. The paintings looked fresh, as if recently painted.

With each step she felt the bitterly cold air growing warmer and warmer. Wherever these people were taking her there was a fire. Finally, she was led into a huge room. At its center was a bonfire with nearly forty people gathered around it—children, babies, parents, elderly men and women. All were wearing animal hides, like her saviors, and a few held long, pointy spears.

Several of the women sprang into action. They escorted Gerdie close to the fire and gave her a crude cup full of an earthy tea. They urged her to drink. The liquid rolled down her throat like lava, warming her to her toes.

"Where am I?" she asked.

The crowd looked at her oddly. It was obvious they did not understand her. Who were they?

And then a theory began to unfold in her mind. Clearly, she had not been teleported as she had intended. Could her ugly little machine actually allow her to travel through time?

And then her heart was racing. "My machine," she said, trying to mime the size and shape of it. "It's out there. I need it!"

The people watched her panic with confused faces. They had no idea what she was saying. They would be no help. She would have to go back out into the snow and get her machine. She couldn't be trapped in the past forever.

Just as she was ready to bolt for the exit, the three warriors who had killed the mammoth came in and joined the crowd. One of them held her machine. Overjoyed, she raced to them. "Oh, thank you! Thank you! You have no idea how important this is to me. It's my only way home and . . ."

The warrior removed her hood and gave Gerdie a shock even more powerful than coming face-to-face with an extinct monster. This "Eskimo" was small with kinky red hair and bad teeth. She had big feet and long arms and legs and a face like a Bigfoot. She looked exactly like Gerdie.

The other two warriors lowered their hoods and Gerdie got another shock. They looked exactly like her sisters, Linda and Luanne. She scanned the cave and quickly picked out a perfect match for her mother. Old Mr. Carlisle from next door was feeding the fire. A carbon copy of her seventh-grade teacher,

Ms. Romis, was hovering nearby. Almost everyone she knew had a twin in that cave.

Dumbfounded, she sat down on the ground and gazed at her invention. It wasn't a teleportation device, and it certainly wasn't a time machine. One look at these people with their familiar faces and she immediately knew what this ugly, backbreaking, wonderful device really did. It had taken her to an alternate reality. She was on another Earth.

She sat pondering what it all meant. Would the government want such a machine? Was there a practical use for it that would win her the money she so desperately needed for her plans?

As she contemplated this, she felt something jabbing her in the foot. She reached down and found a smooth stone beneath her heel. She almost tossed it aside without a glance, but then the firelight glinted off it. She examined it more closely. It was as big as a marble, but each of its crystal facets was clear and flawless.

"This is a diamond," she said to herself, then looked at the hovering crowd of cavepeople. "I found a diamond on the ground. Do you have any idea how much this might be worth?"

The girl that looked just like Gerdie gestured to a corner of the cave. There, lying in a pile, was a heap of diamonds, unwanted, like discarded trash.

Gerdie hopped to her feet, preparing to stuff her pockets to the limit with jewels, when her machine came to life. With its batteries fully charged, the little ball of light appeared and grew. Before she could get her hands on another jewel, there was a flash and she was gone.

A moment later, she found herself back in her room. Out the window she saw angry people. Some were looking under the hoods of stalled cars. Others were pointing at their darkened houses. Gerdie suspected her return was responsible for the blackout, but it was a small price to pay. She had created something the greatest scientific minds could only theorize about. She looked down at the sole shiny diamond she had managed to bring back home, and suddenly, Gerdie Baker wasn't so sure she wanted to sell her ugly old invention any longer.

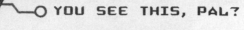
YOU SEE THIS, PAL?

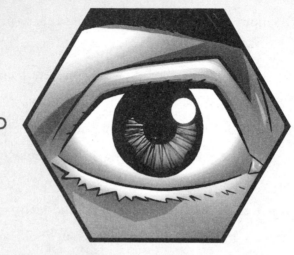

IT'S MY EYE AND IT'S WATCHING YOU.

EVER SINCE WE MADE YOU A FULL-FLEDGED MEMBER OF NERDS, I'VE NOTICED SOME TROUBLING BEHAVIOR FROM YOU AND I'VE COME TO A CONCLUSION . . .

. . . YOU'RE LOSING YOUR MARBLES!

I THINK THE STRESS OF BEING A SECRET AGENT AND A KID IS GETTING TO YOU. YOU LOOK TIRED AND DISTRACTED. IT'S NOTHING TO BE ASHAMED OF—BEING A MEMBER OF THE NATIONAL ESPIONAGE, RESCUE, AND DEFENSE SOCIETY CAN BE DIFFICULT. WHEN I WAS A MEMBER OF THE TEAM, I WAS STRESSED OUT ALL THE TIME. BUT THAT DOESN'T MEAN WE CAN LET THE MENTALLY UNBALANCED STAY ON THE TEAM.

WHO AM I?

HMMM . . . YOU'RE HAVING SOME MEMORY PROBLEMS. THAT'S NOT A GOOD SIGN. MY NAME IS MICHAEL BUCKLEY. I'M A FORMER MEMBER OF NERDS. MY CODE NAME WAS BEANPOLE, AND I WAS THE GREATEST AGENT NERDS EVER SAW.

YES, REALLY!!!!!

ANYWAY, WHEN I RETIRED, I TOOK ON A NEW JOB: DOCUMENTING THE CURRENT TEAM'S CASES AND KEEPING MY GREAT BIG EYE ON NEW RECRUITS. I'VE TALKED TO THE BOSSES ABOUT YOU. WE'RE CONCERNED, SO WE'RE GOING TO GIVE YOU A TEST TO SEE IF YOU ARE MENTALLY FIT TO BE A SECRET AGENT.

WHOA! SLOW DOWN WITH ALL THE QUESTIONS. THE TEST WILL TELL US HOW YOU REACT IN HIGH-PRESSURE SITUATIONS. THE BIG SHOTS WANT TO MAKE SURE BEFORE WE TOSS YOU OFF THE TEAM.

THE TEST IS PRETTY SIMPLE: A SERIES OF MULTIPLE-CHOICE QUESTIONS SIMILAR TO THE TESTS THEY GIVE POLICE OFFICERS, FBI AND CIA AGENTS AND MEMBERS OF THE MILITARY.

HERE'S A SAMPLE QUESTION. ANSWER IT HONESTLY:

1. ARE YOU CRAZY?

a. YES! ABSOLUTELY, YES!
b. KINDA
c. PROBABLY
d. I'M FINE, BUT THE VOICES IN MY HEAD DISAGREE

OK, I'M A LITTLE TROUBLED BY YOUR ANSWER. ARE YOU HIDING SOMETHING? HEY, WHAT'S WITH ALL THE FIDGETING? YOU LOOK NERVOUS. WORSE, YOU LOOK GUILTY! WELL, YOU CAN LIE TO ME, BUT YOU CAN'T LIE TO THE TEST. SO IF YOU HAPPEN TO BE AN AX MURDERER OR A PYROMANIAC, YOU MIGHT AS WELL FESS UP NOW.

HMMM . . . DENIAL. FINE. READ THROUGH THIS CASE FILE AND ANSWER THE QUESTIONS. WHEN YOU'RE FINISHED, WE'LL TOTAL YOUR SCORE TO FIND OUT THE TRUTH.

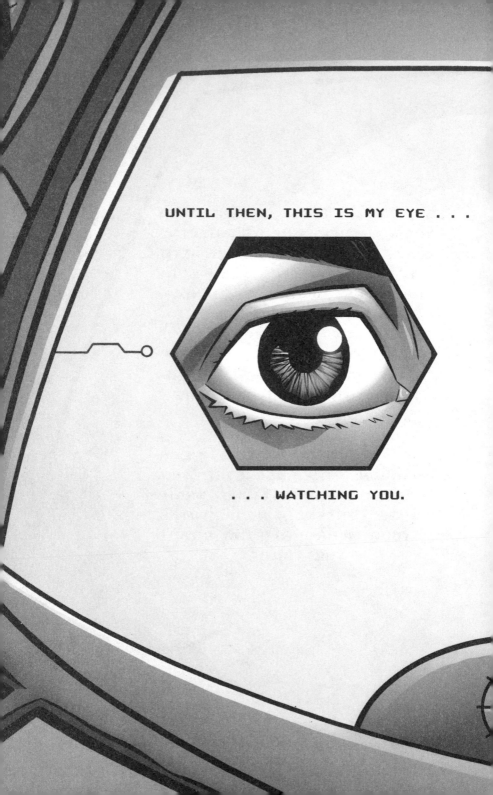

1

Alexander Brand, Nathan Hale Elementary's janitor, limped down the school hallway using his mop wheelie bucket as a makeshift cane. His bad leg was bothering him. Ever since the accident, it ached when a storm was coming. If he could just get off it for an hour or so, it would be as good as new, but he couldn't take a break. His boss wanted to speak with him.

He turned a corner and saw the school's librarian, Ms. Holiday, waiting for him by the supply closet door. She was blonde, with the kind of glasses that made her look both smart and feline. When he saw her, he couldn't help but smile, but he forced it from his face. It wasn't professional. But it was difficult to stay professional when she smiled back.

"If he wants to see us, it must be serious," she said.

Brand nodded. "It's always serious."

He took a set of keys from his coveralls and unlocked the closet door. Once inside, Ms. Holiday turned her attention to a shelf stacked with jugs of bleach and rolls of paper towels. Moving them aside, she placed her hand on the brick wall behind them, and suddenly a pinpoint of green light traced the outline of her fingers.

"Identity scanned and approved. Good morning, Agent Holiday," an electronic voice said.

"Good morning," she replied as Brand unzipped the front of his gray uniform, revealing a surprising sight—an elegant black tuxedo, complete with crisp white shirt and a shiny black tie. He checked his silver cuff links, brushed some lint off his shoulder, and snatched a white cane from the corner.

"How do I look, Ms. Holiday?" he said.

"Dreamy. You know, you can call me Lisa when we're alone, Alexander. After all, we've been dating for almost a month—"

"And we agreed that we were going to keep that a secret. I am your boss."

She put her finger to his lips. "Our secret is safe with me, Agent Brand."

Brand tried to put weight on his cane and stumbled backward. He scowled. He could disarm a nuclear bomb with one arm tied behind his back, but when Holiday was around he became a bumbling idiot.

"Good morning, Director Brand," the electronic voice said.

Brand righted himself. "We're going to the Playground."

"At once," the voice replied. "Delivering in three, two, one."

The floor beneath Brand and Holiday suddenly sank, and the two were sent plummeting deep into the earth aboard a tiny platform. They passed plumbing systems, electric cables, even the remains of an ancient graveyard long lost to history. Soon their platform zoomed into the bowels of a massive cave. Shadows tiptoed along the walls. Water dripped down from above and the air felt cold and thin.

"I can't wait for my secret entrance in the library to be finished. I hate taking this route," Ms. Holiday said as she slipped her hand into Brand's. "It's creepy."

Brand, however, was not frightened. On the contrary, he was fascinated! The cave reminded him of the abandoned mine he and his brother, Tom, had explored as children growing up in Colorado. Their grandfather, who raised them, had warned Tom and Alexander to steer clear of its tunnels, but the boys couldn't help themselves. By the time Tom left home to join the air force, the two brothers knew every twist and turn. Tom would have loved this cave.

"Alexander?"

Brand pulled himself out of his memory. "Yes, Ms. . . . Lisa."

"We're here."

Brand glanced around. He hadn't noticed that the platform had sunk into a room so wide and cavernous it could have doubled as a football field. Columns held up the arched ceiling, each pillar decorated in tiled mosaics celebrating the different areas of science—geology, chemistry, astronomy, and more. Machines filled the vast room, along with hundreds of worktables littered with computer parts, test tubes, circuits, and tools. Scientists in white lab coats bustled about, their hands filled with bizarre instruments and inventions. In the center of the room, a round platform stood a few feet off the ground. On it were five leather chairs surrounding a strange desk. The desk had a small hole cut into it and circuitry embedded beneath its glass surface.

As Brand and Holiday approached the platform, a glowing sphere shot out of the hole in the desk and zipped toward them, stopping within inches of their faces. The sphere was no bigger than a softball and covered in blue blinking lights.

"Welcome to the new and improved Playground, Mr. Brand, Ms. Holiday." The voice came from the blinking sphere.

"Nice to see you again, Benjamin," Ms. Holiday replied.

Unlike the voice in the broom closet, the ball's voice was dignified, proper, and even a little old-fashioned. Benjamin's personality was patterned after one of America's most famous spies, Benjamin Franklin. "What do you think of it?"

"Looks just like the old Playground," Brand said.

"At first glance, yes, but when you take a closer look you will see everything is beyond state-of-the-art—a hundred workstations, a biofueled power grid, and every square inch of wall space can now be adapted for an unlimited number of uses."

The tiles on the walls flipped over and converted into thousands of television monitors broadcasting everything from cartoons to the feed from cameras mounted on ATMs. They could observe every corner of the world from this room.

"Fancy," Ms. Holiday said.

"Indeed," Benjamin said proudly. "It wasn't easy after Heathcliff and Upgrade destroyed the school, but I believe the place will feel like home in no time."

"We have a meeting with General Savage. Could you activate the satellite link?" Ms. Holiday asked.

"Of course," Benjamin said, then emitted a series of clicks. The tiles on the walls flipped over to reveal a giant, bullet-shaped head. Its owner was one General Savage, a battle-hardened soldier who had seen his fair share of wars—a few he had fought all by himself. It was rumored the man could bench-press four hundred pounds and that his earlobes could deadlift twenty pounds apiece. His personality was just as tough.

"Good morning, sir," Brand said.

Savage nodded. "We've got an emergency. Have you got your facility up and running, Director?"

"All the important systems are operational. A little nail pounding won't get in our way," Brand said. "Is there trouble, sir?"

Savage's brows furrowed so deep they nearly covered his eyes. "As you know, NASA satellites monitor the globe. They've found an unusual electrical phenomenon near Akron, Ohio."

"What kind of electrical phenomenon?" Ms. Holiday asked.

"Imagine every flicker of electrical energy being sapped out of every device within a three-block area—no lights, no computers, no instant bank machines. Nothing."

"Are you suspecting sabotage, sir? It could just be a blackout," Brand said.

"Not according to this report." Savage lifted a huge stack of papers, then set them back on his desk with a loud *thump*! "I can't make heads or tails of any of it, so we brought in a scientist. In a nutshell, someone has built some kind of machine that is literally sucking electricity out of the power lines—even pulling it out of batteries. It's happened in seven different locations in Akron, Ohio."

"What kind of a machine needs all that power?" the librarian asked.

"That's your job to find out," the General said. "We don't know who built it or why they are using it, but if they mean to cause chaos for the United States of America, we need to stop them. This device could shut down communication, defense systems, hospitals, the police, banks, grocery stores, everything. Assemble your team, agents."

"They're on a mission, sir," Ms. Holiday said. "But they'll be back soon."

"Well, I hope they're close by. You're going to need all of your resources on this one."

2

"Space . . . the final frontier.
These are the voyages of the starship *Wheezer*. On a five-year mission to seek out new life and new civilizations, and to boldly go where no nerd has gone before!"

With those words, Wheezer pressed the plunger on her inhaler and felt its powerful propulsion system rocket her out into the inky nothingness of space. Her team, the National Espionage, Rescue, and Defense Society, or NERDS, for short, was on a mission to save the International Space Station. They had rocketed through the atmosphere in a superjet, docked with the station, put on high-tech space suits, and were now leaping out of the air lock into nothingness.

Being a secret agent ruled.

"Gruubballla!" Flinch said through the space suit's communication device.

"Anyone want to translate that for me?" Wheezer asked.

"He said enough with the goofing," Pufferfish explained. "He wants to get back to headquarters. He says the lunch lady has made him a special dessert today. Grubberlin . . . or something."

"Gruubballla!" Flinch cried.

"What is Grubberlin?" Braceface asked.

"Who knows? He's had too many juice boxes," Gluestick replied. "After twelve I'm not sure he even knows what he's talking about."

"Flinch, this is the experience of a lifetime, and all you can think about is dessert. Don't tell me you guys are so used to being secret agents that this is boring? What eleven-year-old kid gets to save some astronauts?"

Gluestick's head bobbed in his helmet. "Wheezer's right. This is awesome. What a great opportunity to test out the Z-64 Moon Walk Suits. Each one is specifically designed to work with our unique powers," he said as he strolled along the outside surface of the space station. The chubby boy was the team's resident techno-geek, and he obsessed over anything that blinked and beeped. Wheezer guessed that, for him, wearing a superadvanced space suit made of a flexible, comfy-cozy polymer—completely airtight—was like ten birthdays rolled into one. "My adhesives work just like they would on Earth."

"That's great for you, but my upgrade enhances my allergies and this suit is making me itch!" Pufferfish said, as she tried to scratch her arm through the suit.

"Well, whatever they're made of, they aren't stopping the amazing powers of Braceface," the boy said. His helmet's faceplate acted like a force field, keeping oxygen in but allowing his braces to morph and grow as he willed them. They swirled around in his mouth and produced a superhero statue featuring his own face.

"Gruubballla!" Flinch cried as he beat on his chest like a gorilla.

As the others talked, Wheezer felt her chest tightening. Too much excitement sometimes triggered her asthma. She closed her eyes and focused on the inhalers in her hands. She felt the click that meant the inhalers had switched from rocket boosters to medicine delivery devices. Then she inserted them into the specially designed slots in her helmet. She pushed the plunger and cool mist eased her breathing. She couldn't help but smile. Sure, she had asthma, but here she was on a secret mission in outer space, when less than a year and a half ago she couldn't walk around the block without stopping to catch her breath.

When Matilda "Wheezer" Choi was three years old, she often woke up in the night unable to breathe. She told her parents it felt like an invisible monster was standing on her chest. It wasn't long before a doctor diagnosed her with chronic asthma and prescribed what he called a metered-dose inhaler—a small canister housed inside a plastic plunger—which he said would help. When she put it in her mouth, a premeasured amount of medication was shot directly down her throat into her lungs. It usually made her feel better, but sometimes her attacks were strong and the inhaler was not enough. When her wheezing was really bad, she used a device called a nebulizer, which delivered a powerful mist into her airways. If the inhaler and the nebulizer both failed, Matilda spent the night in the hospital. Some nights as she lay in her hospital bed, looking up at the tiles on the ceiling and wishing her mother and father could sleep by her side, she prayed for a new life—one with sports; field trips; long, uninterrupted nights of sleep; and family pets. But years passed and her prayers went unanswered.

Then one day a Latino boy with a mouth full of licorice approached her. He was shaking so much from the sugar that she could barely understand what he was saying. Then he reached into his shirt and turned a glowing knob on a strange harness covering his body. One twist and he was normal. That was the day she met Flinch. It was also the day she became a secret agent.

Matilda was invited to join a team of kids who all had weaknesses. Flinch was hyperactive. Pufferfish was allergic to everything. Gluestick ate too much paste, and Choppers had the biggest buckteeth she had ever seen. With the help of a supercomputer named Benjamin and special nanobyte technology, each of their weaknesses was turned into a strength. Flinch's hyperactive energy made him superstrong and lightning-fast. Pufferfish's superallergies allowed her to detect lies, danger, and even the tiniest clues at a crime scene. Gluestick's love of adhesives made him a human wall crawler, and Choppers's big teeth allowed him to hypnotize people. Unfortunately, Choppers had turned out to be a criminal mastermind who had betrayed the team. The new fifth member was Braceface, whose monstrous orthodontia could become any tool. And for Matilda, the asthma that had made her feel so powerless became her biggest asset when she was given a pair of inhalers that not only eased her breathing but allowed her to fly. She still had asthma, but now it didn't limit her. Now she was "Wheezer," and nothing could stop her.

"It's time to get to work," Pufferfish said. "There are three astronauts aboard this station, and the last thing they want to see is a bunch of kids goofing off outside the window. As you know, the station has a ruptured oxygen tank. Unfortunately, the onboard computers have gone screwy and can't pinpoint its location. Even worse, all the tanks are linked, so soon they will all be empty. Our job is to find the damaged tank and fix it before they run out of air inside. There are tanks all over the station. Let's split up and find it."

"Hopefully before my lunch is cold!" Flinch said.

Wheezer closed her eyes and concentrated. A quick squeeze and the inhalers were blasters again, sending her flying farther into space like a rocket. She angled toward the far side of the station, marveling at its construction: a series of interconnected pieces that looked like a LEGO set assembled by an alien toddler.

As she neared her section, she immediately spotted a seeping milky gas drifting out of a white tank mounted on the outside of the hull. She pushed a button on the chest plate of her space suit and a cable fired a magnetic tether. It connected to the station's metallic skin and stuck tight. Another button on the chest plate reeled in the slack and soon she was less than a foot from the damage.

"I found our broken tank. It has a big, jagged hole. Not clear what caused it," Matilda said.

Gluestick responded. "Could be anything—pieces of old satellite, rockets, stray meteorites, even a golf ball. There's a lot of junk floating around up here."

"Give me half an hour and I'll have it fixed."

"Don't waste a second," Gluestick said. "That's all the oxygen we have left in our suits. Do you need any help?"

She felt a tap on her shoulder and turned to find Gluestick standing behind her. "How did you get here?"

"I walked," he said, pointing to his feet.

"Are you worried about me, Gluestick?" she said.

"Um, I just didn't see anything, uh, in my section and, ah, I just . . ."

Wheezer smiled. She had a little crush on her teammate. It was nice to see he might feel the same way.

"Activate welding goggles," she said, and a pair of black lenses dropped down from her space helmet. She closed her eyes and concentrated on her hands. There was a soft click in the inhaler and a hot, blue flame ignited at the tip. Through the blackness of her welding goggles she could see its faint flickering, and she went to work on the gaping hole in the air tanks. "This fix is only temporary. These tanks will tear just as easily if something else crashes into them. Perhaps they should build some kind of protective shell."

"I've been talking with NASA all day about it," Gluestick said. "We have technology they won't have for decades. I think it's time we shared."

As Matilda worked, Gluestick kept her company talking about his fascination with space. It was nice to have a conversation with Duncan. Most of their usual interaction involved spy work and filing reports.

All too soon, the tank was sealed. "All done," Matilda said as a little red light flashed on her helmet. "Uh-oh. What's that?"

"That's our oxygen supply," Gluestick said. "Time to go inside, Wheezer."

"All right, all right. Keep your space suit on," Matilda said, but before she could unclasp her tether, she was struck from behind and flung forward. She slammed hard into Gluestick, causing the boy to hit his head on the side of the ship and knocking him unconscious. A meteoroid about the size of an orange floated nerby. Wheezer was surprised that such a small thing could hit so hard. Just then another one flew by and slammed into the ship. She turned to see where it had come from only to spy a small wave of sharp space rocks heading right for them. The station would never survive such an onslaught. She'd be lucky if she could save Gluestick.

"Uh, I've got a problem out here," Matilda said.

"Wheezer, you'd better get back in here," Pufferfish cried. "You and Gluestick only have a couple minutes of air left!"

"I'm a little busy," she said as she aimed her inhalers at a fast-approaching rock. She pulled the trigger. There was burst of light, then an explosion, and in the blink of an eye the meteoroid was vaporized—one down and a hundred to go. Unfortunately,

the rebound force of the blast slammed her and Gluestick into the ship. It hurt, but she had no time to fully recover.

"Gluestick, wake up!" she cried, but got no response. More of the rocks were approaching fast.

She had to stop them, but there was only one way, and it was likely suicide. Without a second thought, Wheezer bravely released her tether and attached it to Gluestick's suit. He was safe. She pressed the plunger on her inhalers and swerved into the path of the approaching meteoroids.

"Bring it," she said, and with another squeeze she flew headfirst into the avalanche, zigzagging between rocks and zapping them one by one as she sailed past. When she broke through the other side of the rock shower, she used her inhalers to spin around and fly back in. She knew she would only get one more shot at saving the station and she had to make it count. So she closed her eyes to concentrate—a nearly impossible task considering the blaring alarm going off in her ears and the dizziness she was feeling from the lack of oxygen. Somehow she managed to will all the nanobytes in her blood to give her inhalers a full charge of energy. The scientists at the Playground had warned her to never bring the nanobytes to their fullest charge. They said the blast could kill her. But what else could she do? Gluestick was in trouble, and so were the astronauts.

She had to save everyone, even if that meant dying herself. So with her hands glowing like two tiny suns, she took aim at the remaining rocks and pushed the plungers on her inhalers. The explosion sent her spinning wildly off course, end over end away from the ship . . . and that's when her air ran out.

3

Heathcliff Hodges was not insane. All you had to do was ask him. Sure, he was angry and irrational and had attacked several of the guards at the Arlington Hospital for the Criminally Insane, but anyone would react that way if they had to sit in group therapy three hours a day learning how to hug. Every day he and a collection of insane misfits talked about their feelings. It was driving him bonkers.

"I almost destroyed the world," Dr. Trouble cried, tears streaming out of the eyeholes of the huge black mask he refused to take off his head. It had big antler-like appendages that were incredibly distracting. They were also prone to poking the other patients in the eyes. "I mean, I was this close! If I could have just

gotten my mystic pyramid to line up correctly with the path of the sun I would have fried the entire Earth like an egg!"

"You'll get another chance," Ragdoll said, patting him on the shoulder. She was annoyingly supportive of the other patients in group therapy, which baffled Heathcliff. Ragdoll had built a machine that turned an entire town into paper dolls. Where was her compassion when half the population of Athens, Georgia, was flattened like a pancake?

"No, I won't!" Dr. Trouble cried. "The sun only aligns in that precise manner every one thousand years. I blew it!"

"You could always clone yourself," said Scanner. His high-tech suit worked like a photocopier, producing unlimited and perfect copies of him. He had used his duplicates to rob banks from Arlington to Dallas. Seemed like a great plan to Heathcliff; unfortunately, the fool had run out of toner during a heist. "Make a copy of yourself and pack it away for a thousand years. That's what I'd do."

Dr. Dozer smiled at the group. "Those are all good ideas, but let me remind you that they are also against the law. Does anyone have any legal ideas that might make Dr. Trouble feel better?"

The room was silent.

Dr. Dozer frowned. "OK, well, we'll work on that next time. For now, I've noticed that Heathcliff hasn't spoken."

"Don't call me that," Heathcliff snarled.

"I'm sorry," the doctor replied. "Would you prefer your other name? Simon?"

"I've given up on that one, too," he said.

"Then what are you calling yourself?"

Heathcliff grimaced. "I haven't decided."

"Well, until then, is there something you'd like to share with the rest of the group?"

Heathcliff looked around the room with disgust. He considered keeping his thoughts to himself but then wondered if getting a few things off his chest might not make him feel better after all.

"I hate all of you!"

"Hey!" Scanner cried. "That's not very positive!"

"Scanner, Heathcliff has a right to express his anger. This is a safe harbor," Ragdoll said.

Heathcliff turned his angry eyes on Ragdoll. "I particularly despise you!"

Ragdoll whimpered.

"I'm losing my mind," he continued. "And yes, I get the irony that this is a mental hospital, but I was perfectly sane when I was dragged in here. Do you know what it's like to sit in my room without any diversions—no books, no television, no explosives! All day and all night I have to listen to my roommate, Chucky Swiller, giggle like an idiot at the boogers he digs out of his nose!"

"Let's be honest. This isn't about your situation. This is about the teeth, isn't it?" Dr. Dozer asked.

Heathcliff frowned. "Yes! My amazing, glorious, magnificent hypnotizing teeth! Knocked out by a lucky punch from one of my bitterest enemies. And now, look at me. I'm powerless. Just some regular kid with a genius-level intelligence—surrounded by morons!"

He hunched down into his chair and tried to avoid their pitying eyes. What he didn't want to tell anyone was that, along with the therapy, the empty space where his teeth had been was driving him crazy. He had developed the habit of poking his tongue in and out of the empty cavern, with its coppery-tasting hole, over and over again. He did it day and night as if his tongue might probe once more and find that his front teeth had suddenly returned from a long summer vacation. He could stand it no longer!

He leaped from his chair and yanked it off the floor. With all his strength he hefted it against a nearby window, which shattered on impact. Heathcliff dashed for it—prepared to cut himself to pieces if it meant escape—but before he even reached the jagged window frame, two hulking guards were on him. Both of the men were easily six foot seven inches tall, all muscle, with shaved heads and sour faces. They wrapped him in a snug straitjacket and shackled his hands and feet with chains that linked into a padlock at his chest. They slipped a hard plastic mask over his face to prevent him from biting anyone, then hoisted him onto a dolly.

"You do realize that when I rule this world you will suffer?" he seethed.

"I believe you've made that clear," one guard said.

"You dare mock me? You will be the first to taste my merciless rage," Heathcliff grumbled.

"Pipe down!" the other guard said. "You've got a visitor."

Heathcliff was rolled into the visitors' room. It wasn't much more than a long hallway lined with cubicles. Each had a chair that faced a thick glass window. Many of the hospital's patients were too dangerous to have direct contact with visitors, so they were separated by the window and communicated by telephone. On the other side was a familiar face—his goon. The man looked like he'd lost a fight. One of his eyes had gone blind and his hair had a peculiar streak of white running down it.

"So," Heathcliff said into the phone his guard held to his ear.

The goon tried to pick up his phone, but one of his hands was nothing but a metal hook. He struggled with the receiver and it fell out of his steel claw seven times before Heathcliff lost his patience.

"Use the other hand, you fool!"

The phone was attached to a plastic cord that was very short. To wrap it around to his other ear the goon nearly had to strangle himself.

"What do you want?" Heathcliff barked but suddenly

38°86' N, 77°07' W

wished he could take it back. The goon had a reputation as a man who liked to break bones. Heathcliff suddenly worried that the thick glass between them might not be thick enough.

"I got good news fer ya, boss."

"Tell me you're going to get me out of here," Heathcliff begged. He was so excited the phone fell from his shoulder onto the desk. The guard stared at it indifferently. Heathcliff leaned over so that his ear was near the receiver.

The goon shook his head. "Can't do it, boss. This place is tighter than a drum. They've got guards guarding the guards. Never seen anything like it. You know they only put the most dangerous screwballs in here." The goon paused. "I'm sorry, I didn't mean to say you was a screwball."

"If you can't free me, how could anything you've come to say be considered good news?"

"I delivered the present."

"The present? What are you talking about?"

"The box and the letter! Ya know, the one you gave me in case of dire consequences. You said to give it to Gertrude Baker if you ever got arrested. Her mom moved her to Ohio, but I got it to her."

Heathcliff grinned as he remembered. "If I wasn't in a straitjacket, I would hug you! Good news, indeed. Do you know what was in the box and the letter?"

The goon looked offended. "As a goon, I take my employer's privacy very serious. It's sorta an unwritten rule of the profession."

"Well, you would have hardly understood it, but that present will destroy the world."

"How is that good news, boss?" the goon said.

"Because if Gerdie Baker is as smart as I remember, she's going to build a machine so dangerous they'll be forced to let me out so I can stop her. Screwball will soon be free!"

"Screwball? I thought you were calling yourself Simon."

"If the world thinks I'm crazy, who am I to argue?" Screwball said, then a sudden giggling fit came over him. It went on and on.

"Wow, boss, that laugh is creepy," the goon said.

"You like it?" Screwball asked. "I've been working on it for a while. I think it has the right combination of foreboding and madness. New name! New laugh! New doomsday plot to destroy the world!"

Then he laughed again.

"Real creepy, boss."

END TRANSMISSION.

ALL RIGHT, LET'S GET THIS TEST STARTED. THE LESS TIME I'M ALONE WITH YOU THE BETTER!

BEFORE WE GET STARTED, YOU NEED TO VERIFY YOUR IDENTITY, SO PLEASE ENTER YOUR CODE NAME BELOW.

_____

HEE-HEE. I FORGOT HOW FUNNY THAT CODE NAME IS . . . GIVE ME A SECOND. OH BOY! I HAVEN'T LAUGHED THAT HARD IN YEARS.
I NEARLY WET MYSELF.

OK, NO MORE GOOFING OFF.
LET'S GET TO THE TEST.

TO ACCURATELY DEDUCE YOUR MENTAL STATE, IT IS IMPORTANT THAT YOU ANSWER EACH QUESTION HONESTLY. EVEN IF THOSE ANSWERS MAY MAKE YOU APPEAR TO BE A LOONY-TUNE, YOU STILL MUST ANSWER AS CLOSE TO THE TRUTH AS POSSIBLE.

EACH QUESTION IS MULTIPLE-
CHOICE AND HAS FOUR POSSIBLE
ANSWERS, WHICH IS WHY WE CALL
IT A MULTIPLE-CHOICE TEST, DUH!
SEE, NOW YOU'RE CATCHING ON. . . .
LET'S BEGIN.

1. WHEN PEOPLE DON'T LISTEN
TO YOUR IDEAS, WHAT DO YOU DO?

a. CRY (3 POINTS)
b. POUT AND STOMP FEET (2 POINTS)
c. BREAK SOMETHING (5 POINTS)
d. PLOT THEIR DEATHS (10 POINTS)

2. ARE PEOPLE TALKING ABOUT
YOU BEHIND YOUR BACK?

a. OF COURSE THEY ARE! (3 POINTS)
b. NO, THEY ARE TALKING ABOUT ME
IN FRONT OF MY FACE (2 POINTS)
c. NOT SO MUCH TALKING BUT LOTS OF
WHISPERING (6 POINTS)
d. WHO CAN HEAR THEM WITH ALL THE
VOICES IN MY HEAD? (10 POINTS)

3. WHAT DO YOU WANT TO BE WHEN YOU GROW UP?

a. LORD AND MASTER OF ALL I SEE (7 POINTS)
b. MAD SCIENTIST (5 POINTS)
c. WICKED STEPMOTHER (4 POINTS)
d. AMBASSADOR TO OUR ALIEN CONQUERORS (10 POINTS)

4. WHAT DO YOU WEAR ON A TYPICAL DAY?

a. A MASK TO HIDE MY HORRIBLY DISFIGURED FACE (8 POINTS)
b. A CAPE, MONOCLE, AND WALKING STICK (4 POINTS)
c. A TINFOIL HAT TO BLOCK MIND READERS (10 POINTS)
d. A STRAITJACKET (10 POINTS)

5. WHICH WOULD MAKE YOU THE MOST AFRAID?

a. A DARK ROOM (3 POINTS)
b. A CONFINED SPACE (3 POINTS)

c. HEIGHTS (2 POINTS)
d. FRIED CHICKEN
   (10 POINTS)

OK, NOW ADD UP THE POINTS
AND WRITE THE TOTAL HERE.

_____

EGAD! THAT'S A HIGH NUMBER. OK,
DON'T PANIC. LET'S JUST MOVE
ON. KEEP READING THIS CASE
FILE WHILE I CALL A DOCTOR,
OR THE POLICE, OR A SWAT TEAM.

ACCESS GRANTED

BEGIN TRANSMISSION:

4

Gerdie carefully placed ten hot water bottles on her bed, then eased herself on top of them. She had never been so sore in her life and she knew why— the machine. She had been lugging it all over town for a week. Every time she turned it on, it sucked all the electricity out of the surrounding area, so she was constantly forced to find new locations to draw power. She guessed that the machine needed the energy to open the doorways to other worlds, but she couldn't wrap her head around the math to fully understand. Once upon a time, her brain had been upgraded with nanobyte technology. Back then there was no mystery she couldn't solve. Oh well. She was still smart enough to make herself beautiful.

"We've both been working hard, and it's time for our

reward," she said to the machine, which was propped up next to her bed. "We're both getting makeovers! I'm getting the works and you're going to get smaller and lighter. I know that our real beauty is on the inside, but who can see it through all these layers of ugly?"

She gingerly sat up and scooped her phone off the nightstand. She tapped a few numbers into the keypad and waited for someone to answer.

"Hello, this is the medical office of Thompson and Chase, Plastic Surgeons. How can I help you?"

"I'd like to make an appointment," Gerdie said.

"Very good," the receptionist said. "And exactly what procedure are you interested in?"

Gerdie eyed herself in her mirror. "You name it."

"OK," the receptionist said. "And can you give me your insurance information?"

"No need," Gerdie replied as she gazed around her room. It was filled with golden statues, great works of art, buckets of jewels, and exotic furs she had shoplifted during her trips to other worlds. "I'll be paying in cash."

5

Matilda's eyes fluttered open.

"Gluestick! Is he alive? And what about the space station? Did I save it from the meteoroids?!"

"She's gone crazy," a voice said. "If we have to send her away, I get her room."

Matilda looked around and found she was not in outer space but in her own bedroom, surrounded by her six older brothers: Marky, Max, Michael, Moses, Mickey, and Mobi.

"Who says?" Moses cried.

"I'm the biggest. I need the space," Mickey shouted. "I should get the room."

"I'm the oldest," Marky declared. "I've suffered the longest."

"No one is getting my room," Matilda said, but they weren't

listening. As usual, the boys' argument turned into a wrestling match, and six sets of legs and arms thumped around the room, carelessly jostling her prized possessions: her autographed photos of Muhammad Ali and Triple H, her authentic WWE World Heavyweight Championship Belt, a framed photograph of herself in the Ultimate Fighting octagon as her opponent tapped out. She leaped to her feet and stood over the boys with fists clenched. "If you losers break anything, I will deliver a world of hurt that you will never recover from."

The boys stared at her for a moment, laughed, then went back to their battle royal. Enraged, she leaped into the crowd and joined the fight.

"ENOUGH!" a voice cried. Their mother had entered the room, and from her tone, she was angry. The fighting stopped and the seven Choi children lay on the floor, breathing hard and staring up at their mother like she was a four-star general.

Matilda's mother's real name was Mi-sun, but she went by Molly. She was small in stature, with long dark hair and murky brown eyes. When she smiled, she was like a flower opening for the first time, but when she was angry, she looked more like a dragon with smoke escaping from her nose.

"You're lucky Mom showed up," Mobi muttered.

"When I was finished with you guys, the tooth fairy would have had to file for bankruptcy!" Matilda whispered back.

"Boys, disappear," Molly said. "I want to see how your sister is feeling and you are making her crazy."

When her brothers were gone, Molly crossed the room and stopped at the window. Resting on the sill was a *hareubang*: a small stone creature shaped like a totem pole with a mushroom hat. It had bulging eyes and a kindly smile. Molly had given Matilda the statue for "protection." It was supposed to ward off evil spirits. Unfortunately, it had no power over her brothers, unless, of course, she threw it at them.

"The lunch lady from school brought you home yesterday. You've been asleep ever since," Molly said. "She is a very odd lady with a very deep voice. What were you doing at school? It's summer vacation."

Matilda gulped. What was she supposed to say? *I live a double-life as a secret agent? I have superpowers? My school has a secret headquarters in the basement? The lunch lady isn't really a lunch lady but a spy who flies a rocket hidden under the gym floor? And . . . he's not really a lady?*

"I'm taking summer classes," Matilda lied. "If I want to get into a good college, I have to get ahead."

"You are eleven!" Molly said. "College is a long way off."

Matilda could see the doubt in her mother's face. Molly's suspicions were growing daily. Her mom knew nothing about

Matilda's secret life—only her explanations about "after-school sports" and "detentions"—but she wasn't dumb. Too many times Matilda's two worlds had collided, and it was just a matter of time before her second life as a secret agent would be revealed.

She watched her mom pick up the stone idol. "What do you think, old grandfather? Old grandfather sees everything, Matilda. He looks after you and grants wishes. Your grandmother gave him to me before I moved to America with your father. We wished for a baby. Clearly, it works. In fact, I may have to send old grandfather away. No more babies, old grandfather.

"Someday, he will help you when it is your time to lead this family."

"Mother!"

Molly laughed. Her ancestors were from a small island at the southern tip of South Korea called Jeju-do. Molly had told Matilda the island had three things in abundance: rocks, wind, and women. Women, like Matilda's grandmother, Tammora, were the heads of households. They managed the families and the finances and made most of the decisions in the local government. Molly had been raised to do the same. It seemed to work in their family, as Matilda's father was a scatterbrained artist who couldn't balance his checkbook.

"Your brothers tease you, but eventually they will look to

you for guidance. They will need it, too. A few of them are knuckleheads—sweet, lovable, but knuckleheads. But I worry about you, little M. You live a life of mystery, and your words are thick with secrets. Sometimes you tell me things that are not true."

Matilda looked out the window rather than meet her mother's gaze.

"I should punish you . . . but I believe there is an important reason behind your lies. Perhaps you fight evil like old grandfather? He chases off devils, dark creatures, monsters, and invaders from other worlds."

"More Old Grandfather, Molly?" a voice said from the doorway. Matilda turned to see her father, Ben Choi. Though his ancestors were from Korea, he had grown up in San Francisco. Ben met Molly when he visited her island. He saw her in the street and asked to take her picture. It was love at first snapshot. But lately things had been tense. Matilda's parents had been arguing for months. "How are you, pea pod?"

"I'm fine, really!" Matilda said. "Maybe old grandfather can tell me how to get my parents to stop arguing?"

Molly set the stone guardian back in its place on the windowsill and turned to Ben. "Have you had breakfast?"

He shook his head.

"Good, then you can cook," Molly said.

Ben laughed.

Matilda's heart filled with hope. They were the first smiles she had seen on her parents' faces in a long time. Just then she let loose a sneeze so strong it ruffled her blankets. Matilda frowned. She didn't have a cold. Her sneeze was caused by the comlink implant in her nose. It wasn't long before she could hear Agent Brand's voice in her ear.

"Wheezer, we have an emergency mission. Can you get to the roof?"

"The roof? Right now?" Matilda grumbled.

Her mother cocked an eyebrow then turned to her father. "The child is so odd. She speaks to herself. I blame you. You have crazies on your side of the family."

Her dad frowned. "You're the one talking to statues."

Matilda led them both to her door. "I'm really not feeling well enough for breakfast. I'll just go back to bed, but you two go have some fun."

"We gave up fun about seven kids ago," Ben said.

Matilda ushered them into the hall then closed the door. She quickly changed into a black shirt and a pair of neon purple pants, then pulled on her favorite pair of combat boots. She took a quick peek in the mirror. Her hair was a little too neat, so she messed it up until she looked like she had been mugged. Perfect!

She opened her bedroom window and climbed out on to the trellis that led to the roof. There she found a rope ladder hanging down from above. She looked up and saw a big yellow jet plane hovering silently over her home. She climbed the rope rung by rung and found the school bus at the top. Agent Brand pulled her into the ship.

"I hope you know I'm skipping a very important breakfast with my parents for this," she said.

"Sorry if saving the world got in the way of your Rice Krispies," he replied.

Matilda sighed. No one knew her troubles at home. For so long she had hoped her parents' fighting would go away. Now it seemed to be getting worse. Her only real break from it came from her work as a spy.

She strapped herself into her seat just as the ship aimed its nose toward the heavens. With an ear-popping blast, its engines shot them all into the stratosphere. She looked over and noticed Duncan sitting beside her. She gave him a smile and got one back.

"Thanks for saving my life," he said.

"You're welcome. Who saved mine?"

"That would be me," Jackson said from his seat behind them. "I used my braces to cling to the ship and found you floating around like a rubber ducky in a bathtub. Thank-yous can be sent as cash gifts."

Matilda laughed. "What's the big, important mission now?"

Pufferfish shrugged. "All I know is we're going to Akron, Ohio."

"Akron, Ohio? What could possibly happen there?"

"If the reports are true, it's something very unsettling," Agent Brand said. "I'll let the chief of police explain."

Ten minutes later the ship was rocketing back through the atmosphere. Ms. Holiday opened the hatch, then handed the children their parachutes. Matilda was the first to leap out into the sky, and she studied Akron from above. It seemed utterly ordinary—not the kind of place that needed the assistance of a team of superspies.

She landed a block from a police station. Her teammates followed, and together they gathered their gear before anyone noticed them. At the station, Wheezer spotted a handwritten sign taped to the front door. It explained that the station was currently without electricity.

Pufferfish showed the desk sergeant her badge. Not many people had ever seen a National Espionage, Rescue, and Defense

Society I.D., and the police officer laughed. "This is a joke, right? Hey, everybody, the federal agents they sent are here. Do we have any juice boxes?"

The officer nearly fell over laughing.

"You're kids?" a portly man said as he entered the room. "Oh, well, it's not the craziest thing I've seen today. I'm Chief Chris Churchill. I'll show you the . . . um, problem."

He escorted the team into the basement lockup using only a flashlight.

"So you kids are spies, huh?"

"Sorry, you don't have security clearance high enough to know that," Wheezer said.

Chief Churchill shrugged. "Listen, I'm going to warn you. What we have down here is a bit on the weird side. I've got a couple officers who have had to take the day off to get over it."

"It's a monster, isn't it?" Flinch said, rubbing his hands together in satisfaction.

"You'll have to judge that for yourself," Churchill said as he led them into a small office where three dogs—a golden retriever, a poodle, and a Chihuahua—were held in a cage.

"This is what has gotten you so worked up, Chief?" Matilda asked. "Are you afraid of fleas?"

"Listen, kids, we found them wandering the streets and thought they were a bunch of strays until . . ."

THE CHEERLEADERS OF DOOM

Suddenly, Matilda got the shock of her life.

"Let me out of here. I have my rights!" the golden retriever cried.

"No way!" shouted Braceface.

"Incredible!" Gluestick said.

"Better than monsters!" Flinch laughed.

"You can't keep us," the Chihuahua barked. "I'm a lawyer. I'll sue you for every penny you have."

"I demand a phone call!" the poodle cried.

Pufferfish bent down to get a closer look at the dogs. "Um, how did you get so smart?"

The retriever snarled. "What kind of a stupid question is that?"

"Dogs don't talk," she said.

"Yeah, on what planet?" the poodle barked.

"This one," Matilda replied. The whole conversation was making her feel nauseated. "Are you part of some secret experiment?"

The poodle stepped forward. "Kid, I'm an accountant. I got a boyfriend, and he's probably worried about me."

"Are you saying you came from some place where all dogs can talk? How did you get here?"

The Chihuahua whined. "There was this light, then this tearing sound, and then all of a sudden you people are staring at us like we're freaks in a carnival."

"Are they saying you came from another world?" Pufferfish asked.

"I'm not saying anything," the retriever responded. "You're saying that. We're from Earth, a place where all dogs talk—cats, too! And a few squirrels and fish. What's this place called?"

Matilda turned back to face her team. They all had the same stunned expression. "Chief, if you've had any other weird events in this town lately, we'd like to hear about them."

SUPPLEMENTAL MATERIAL

The following transcripts were provided by Chief Chris Churchill and the city of Akron, Ohio. They document interviews between police officers and the family of one missing person: Gertrude (Gerdie) Baker. Linda Baker (sister), Luanne Baker (sister), and Wendy Baker (mother) reported Gerdie missing.

Officer: When was the last time you saw Gerdie?

Linda: Easy. She came down to the backyard yesterday to ruin our lives!

Officer: Pardon?

Luanne: We were in the backyard practicing for the NCA Junior All-Star tryouts when—

Officer: NCA?

Luanne: Cheerleading! Geez, don't you know anything? The National Cheerleading Association. The tryouts for one of the national squads are in a few days!

Officer: OK. How did she ruin your lives?

Linda: She came out in her crazy costume right in the middle of our pyramid.

Officer: Huh?

Wendy: A pyramid is a cheerleading stunt where the girls stack on top of one another. It's shaped liked a—

Officer: I know what a pyramid is! What was the costume?

Luanne: She came down in one of our cheerleading outfits and her freak mask.

Wendy:	It's not a freak mask, girls.
Luanne:	That's what you've been calling it behind her back.
Wendy:	Luanne, that . . . um . . . that's not true.
Linda:	Yes it is. You said it five seconds before the cops showed up.
Officer:	Freak mask?
Wendy:	Gerdie recently had some cosmetic surgery, and her face has been wrapped in bandages for the last four weeks.
Linda:	So she should be easy to find. Just look for a girl who looks like a mummy wearing a cheerleading outfit.
Luanne:	And the big machine strapped to her back. That should be easy to spot.
Officer:	Big machine?
Linda:	Yes, it had these big tubes and all these lights. It looked like it weighed a ton.
Officer:	What kind of game are you playing?
Wendy:	Excuse me?
Officer:	You know there's a lot of crime out there in this city. We've had these crazy blackouts that are causing all kinds of problems. You can't call the police with some silly story—
Wendy:	We're not making this up! She's wearing a cheerleading outfit. Her face is wrapped in bandages. She's got something as big as a trash can tied to her back.
Luanne:	You have to take this seriously. She ruined our lives. I want you to find her, arrest her, and

make her break rocks in jail.

Officer: OK, let's just assume what you're telling me isn't the result of a gas leak in your home. How did this disfigured cheerleader ruin your lives?

Linda: She scared the pyramid. Everyone fell. My sister broke her collarbone. I have a sprained ankle. Everyone on the squad was injured. We'll never make one of the national squads now. We might even lose our spots on the local team!

Luanne: Plus, she stood over us and said the harshest things. She said we were a lousy family. She said we were jerks and she was going to the NCA tryouts herself to take our spots. Then she said we weren't pretty enough to be cheerleaders!

Linda: That's just mean!

Officer: OK, I think I've heard enough.

Wendy: So you have enough information to find my daughter?

Officer: No, but I have enough information to have the three of you arrested. You have the right to remain silent and I suggest you embrace that right. Anything you say can and will be used against you in a court of law—

Linda: Hey, we're telling the truth.

Officer: Calm down—

Wendy: Get off me!

Luanne: Get your hands off my mom.

Officer: I'm warning you, lady—

Luanne: Hit him with a lawn chair!

At this point, the officer fired his Taser three times, incapacitating the Bakers. They were arrested for assault and filing a false crime report. All three were being held in the Summit County Jail.

If Gerdie Baker actually exists, her whereabouts are unknown.

SEE ATTACHED COMPOSITE DRAWING OF "GERDIE BAKER."

6

38°53' N, 77°05' W

Matilda and the NERDS returned to the Playground to make their report. With talking dogs, radiation spots, blackouts, and psychotic cheerleaders, Matilda could barely make sense of the evidence, so she was stunned when Ruby said she knew who had caused it all.

"Her code name was Mathlete," Ruby said. "She was one of us."

"Back up," Matilda said. "How do you know it was a member of NERDS responsible for all this weird stuff?"

"The Mathlete's real name was Gerdie Baker," Ruby said.

"The missing girl with the plastic surgery!" Matilda said.

"Gerdie? She can't be responsible for this," Ms. Holiday said. "She was always so sweet."

Ruby shook her head. "I'm afraid the evidence says otherwise. While you were talking to dogs, Benjamin and I dug up everything we could on Gerdie—history, case files, recent actions . . . Benjamin?"

The little blue orb hovered over the hole in the glass desk. Clicking and spinning, it projected a moving hologram of a very awkward young girl. She was fighting off a team of ninja assassins with gleaming swords in their hands. They rushed at her, but the girl matched their assault fist for fist. Without warning, her attackers flew backward and hit the wall, where they crumbled like children's toys.

"I like her style!" Matilda said.

Benjamin chirped. "Team, this is Gertrude Baker, formerly code-named Mathlete. Her talent was with equations, and her upgrades allowed her brain to process complex problems at lightning speed."

"What kind of a lousy upgrade is that?" Matilda asked.

"Lame!" Jackson agreed.

Ruby shook her head. "With her supercalculator head she could predict the actions of her opponents and exploit their weaknesses. She could also calculate the correct balance and leverage needed to move impossibly heavy things."

An image appeared of the girl leaping onto a beam jammed underneath a car. The car popped up and flipped several times.

"OK, that was cool," Flinch said.

"Math made her into a superhero," Duncan said. "So why'd she leave?"

"Her mother moved the family to Ohio when she divorced Gertrude's father," Ms. Holiday said. "Like many members of the team, her parents were unaware of her secret life. Parents in the dark sometimes make decisions for their children that take them away from us. Gerdie's nano improvements were removed, and Matilda was brought in to be her replacement."

"I was her replacement?" Matilda asked.

"Indeed. Though it appears she has continued to use her superior math skills," Benjamin said.

"And they've led her to a life of crime," Agent Brand said, joining the meeting with a stack of files under his arm. "We're certain she's behind the chaos in Ohio."

Ms. Holiday gasped. "Alexander, I only met her once, but I can't believe she would do such a thing."

"How many thought the same of Heathcliff Hodges? Now he's in a mental hospital for the criminally insane."

"Actually, I had my suspicions about him," Jackson said.

"I'm sorry, Ms. Holiday, but Mr. Brand is right," Duncan said. "From what I've read, Gerdie is the only person in Akron—maybe even in North America—who has the brainpower to create a device that steals electricity. Though all that electricity is probably being used to power something else—something a lot more danger-ous. I believe she's messing around with the multiverse."

"Huh?" Flinch asked.

"The multiverse," Duncan said. "Didn't you guys read Bartlett's Quantum Irregularities paper in *Scientific American* magazine?"

"Sorry, I must have missed that one," Jackson said.

"I'll try to simplify it as much as possible," Ms. Holiday said. "You've all heard of the universe, correct?"

"Sure," Matilda offered. "The universe is everything—Earth, the moon, the stars, forever and ever."

"That's right, Wheezer," Ms. Holiday said. "The universe is everything. Now imagine there was another 'everything.' Imagine there was another Earth, and moon, and stars—existing in the exact same place, only in a different dimension. Imagine it had people and animals and oceans and land."

"Two Earths?" Pufferfish said.

"More than just two. Imagine there are thousands, millions, even billions of universes like ours—only in their own dimensions. Benjamin, could you be so kind as to visually demonstrate?"

Benjamin projected a holographic image of Earth before their eyes. Then it duplicated the image. Then again, and again, and again, until the copies filled the entire room.

Matilda could barely wrap her head around the idea. "Exactly like ours?"

Ms. Holiday shook her head. "Not exactly, and that's where the multiverse gets interesting. Some of these Earths are a lot like ours, while some you wouldn't even recognize."

"I have to admit I'm a bit lost," Agent Brand said.

"Think of it like this," Ms. Holiday told them. From her handbag she took two candy bars, which she placed in front of Flinch on the desk. "Flinch has two candy bars. He can choose to eat the coconut-peanut bar here or he can choose the one made from nougat and honey. Which one does he choose?"

Flinch looked distressed. It was clear that making this choice was probably the hardest thing he had ever had to do in his short life. His head went back and forth from one treat to the other, like he was watching a tennis match, until he finally snatched the coconut bar. He tore open its packaging and ate it greedily.

"So Flinch made a choice and the rest of his life will move forward according to that choice. But the multiverse allows for other possibilities. If the theory is correct, there is another Flinch, in another universe, in another dimension, where he chose the nougat-and-honey candy bar."

"Who cares which candy bar he ate?" Matilda said. "What difference will it make?"

"Very little, probably," Ms. Holiday replied. "But sometimes the decisions are much bigger and have much wider consequences. In the multiverse there's an Earth where the Germans won World War II. There's an Earth where Native Americans still control this continent. There's probably even an Earth where everyone is a pro wrestler."

"Awesome," Matilda said.

"Is there an Earth out there where I ate both candy bars?" Flinch asked, eyeing the other treat.

Ms. Holiday giggled. "Yes. There could even be one where you didn't eat them. Maybe you had carrots and hummus instead."

"I assure you there is not," Flinch said, licking his fingers. "There might be a trillion versions of me, but not one of them would pick carrots and hummus over a chocolate bar."

"There might be a Flinch who is allergic to peanuts and coconut and got very sick from eating the candy bar. There's one where he is a donkey who likes candy. Another, where he was never born. Still another, where candy was never invented, and so on and so on. All of them exist—they are real—on their own Earths, at least according to the theory. Do you understand?"

"Sure, I get it," Pufferfish said. "There are a billion different me's, some good, some bad, some that don't swell up like a balloon whenever I eat eggs. What does this have to do with Mathlete and her machine?"

Duncan stepped forward. "We can't be sure until we question her, but I believe she's using some sort of device that builds a bridge from our world into those alternate Earths."

"Someone's been watching too much *Star Trek*!" Matilda said. "Even if she did build something like that—why? What would she gain from it?"

"We think we know," Benjamin said. The tiles on the walls flipped over to reveal a massive television screen displaying Gerdie Baker's face. "Four weeks ago Mathlete visited a dentist. She ordered a set of porcelain veneers for her teeth and had her jaw fractured to correct an unfortunate under-bite. The procedures in total cost nearly thirty-five thousand dollars."

"So maybe her mother got a good job or won the lottery," Jackson said.

"According to this report, Gerdie didn't pay with money. She paid with this." Brand snapped his fingers and the image changed from sad Gerdie Baker to an ancient treasure chest overflowing with gold coins, pearls, and silver chalices.

Flinch stuffed the other candy bar into his mouth. "Where did she get that?"

"Certainly not from around here. This was found with it," Benjamin said as one of the coins zoomed into focus. On it was a picture of a strange animal with the head of an owl, the body of a bear, and a long tail like a snake. The creature was wearing a crown. An inscription read, *Coin of the Realm. His Royal Highness Doogan the Fifth, King of Zedavia and Surrounding Realms.*

"Zedavia?" Matilda asked. "I've never heard of the kingdom of Zedavia."

"That's because it didn't exist—at least not on our world. I've researched every history book in our database," Ms. Holiday said. "If it was a real place, I would be able to find it. I may be a spy, but I'm a librarian, too."

Gerdie's face came back onscreen, and Brand continued. "A week later, Ms. Baker went to a dermatologist where she was given a laser dermabrasion procedure and a facial and pore treatment that cost nearly two thousand bucks. She ordered a package of ten spray-on tans and a tea bag massage. She paid with this."

An image of a painting appeared on the screen. It looked a lot like the *Mona Lisa.*

"She stole the *Mona Lisa* out of the Louvre?" Matilda asked.

"This isn't the *Mona Lisa*. Look closer," Benjamin chirped as the image zoomed in on the famous painting.

Matilda studied the portrait. It was the same painting she had seen a million times in books. But when she peered closer, she saw something peculiar in the background: silver half-moon–shaped crafts hovering in the sky shooting lasers down on the countryside below.

"An alien invasion!" Matilda said.

"Some idiot painted a copy and added a joke," Ruby said.

Mr. Brand shook his head. "No, we've had art historians study the brushstrokes. This painting was made by Leonardo da Vinci—or at least *a* Leonardo da Vinci. We found a strand of a brush in the paint and had it tested for age. It dates back to the sixteenth century. The signature is also an exact duplicate."

"There's more," Benjamin said. "The next day, Ms. Baker had a consultation with Dr. Abigail Contessa, a plastic surgeon to the stars in Los Angeles. The day after that she received fifty thousand dollars worth of procedures, including a nose job, collagen injections in her lips, a brow lift, and an ear tuck."

"You can do that?" Duncan said as he self-consciously tugged on his lobes.

"Let me guess," Jackson said. "She paid with something that shouldn't exist?"

Brand nodded and live video of an odd bird appeared on the screen. It had gray feathers, thick yellow talons, and a large beak shaped like the end of a wooden spoon.

"It's a dodo," Ms. Holiday said. "Dodos have been extinct for nearly three hundred years."

"So Gerdie Baker is stealing from alternate worlds to pay

for makeovers," Matilda said. "What do we do? We don't have jurisdiction over the multiverse."

"It's much worse than some interdimensional shoplifting," Agent Brand said. "There have been what we've come to call 'crossovers.' Things have been coming into our world—things that should not be here."

"Like the talking dogs?" Duncan asked.

"Worse," Brand said.

The screen showed four strange creatures with black tentacles all over their faces. Though shaped like men, each had a wide wound of a mouth filled with sharp, pointy teeth. They were locked in a jail cell, shouting angrily.

"OK," Jackson said. "I'm officially freaked out."

"That's just the beginning," Brand said.

Matilda's mind filled with worst-case scenarios. "So we track down Mathlete and arrest her."

"Not so simple," Mr. Brand said. "She's had extensive work done on her face, and her doctors are reluctant to talk to us. Performing plastic surgery on a minor is unethical. Who knows if her face would have changed naturally as she got older? Besides, the doctors only saw her swollen face when she left their offices. Mathlete never came back for her follow-ups."

"We don't know what she looks like?" Pufferfish asked.

"No one knows what she looks like. Not even her mother and sisters—as you know, she ran away from home."

Matilda rolled her eyes. Why would someone have surgery to change their appearance? She liked how she looked, and who cared what other people thought of it?

"Let me get this straight," Jackson said. "We're searching for someone who has been trained as a spy. We have no idea what she looks like. If we find her, she has a machine that lets her escape into other worlds."

Brand nodded.

"Grubblin-oogh!" Flinch said, pounding on his chest. The sugar from the candy was coursing through him.

"We do think we have a lead," Brand said. "The National Cheerleading Association is hosting several week-long camps for its elite performers that end with a national competition here in D.C. We believe Gerdie has tried out and made one of the junior teams and is now practicing at one of the camps. Based on more strange electrical activity, we think we know which camp."

"The bad guy is a cheerleader?" Jackson asked.

"Aren't they all?" Matilda said. "I hate cheerleaders with their stupid skirts and phony smiles. I don't know how anybody could have such little self-respect to cheer for a bunch of muscle-heads throwing a ball around. Well, I'm going to enjoy this mission!

We go to the camp, figure out which one is Gerdie, then lay the smackdown on her! Better yet, we lay the smackdown on the entire squad until one of them confesses, and I get to try out a few new submission holds. Everyone wins!"

Brand shook his head. "There will be no laying of the smack. We're thinking something subtler than a steel-cage match. One of you is going undercover. The rest will act as information and tactical support."

"Awesome! I always wanted to go undercover. I finally get to be James Bond," Jackson said.

"Not you, Jackson."

"What?? I'm perfect for this! I'm the most charming, I wear clothes that fit—"

"Unless you want to wear a skirt and a wig, I don't think this job is right for you," Ms. Holiday said.

The lunch lady overheard as he passed through the lab and grunted angrily.

"This camp is girls-only. The perfect agent for this assignment is Matilda," Agent Brand said.

"Me?"

"Yes. You're going to become a competitive cheerleader."

Matilda stared at Brand and Holiday like they were speaking a different language.

"I can't be a cheerleader!" Matilda cried. "Didn't you just

hear me? I hate cheerleaders! Besides, if you haven't noticed, I'm nothing like a cheerleader. They have to be nice and friendly and full of positive energy. I have season tickets to the monster truck rally. I arm-wrestle college students for money every Saturday in the park. I spend my free time analyzing Ultimate Fighting. I'm not cheerleader material."

"Plus, she's a spaz," Jackson said.

Matilda reached for Jackson and put him in a headlock. He struggled but could not free himself. "See what I just did? Do cheerleaders put their friends into choke holds?"

"Agent Wheezer!" Brand bellowed before Ms. Holiday interrupted him.

"Matilda, you are the most agile member of the team—cheerleaders have to be agile. You are also the most fearless—and cheerleaders have to be fearless."

"You are also loud and obnoxious. You're perfect for this mission," Flinch argued.

"You want to be in a choke hold, too? Send Pufferfish!"

"I'm allergic to pom-poms," Ruby said, scratching at her arm. "And organized sports and . . . being peppy. And talking about organized sports and being peppy."

Matilda released Jackson's head. "If you haven't noticed, I'm like leader of the tomboys."

"We're bringing someone in who can help," Brand said. "She'll teach you all the moves."

"It's going to take more than that," Jackson said. "She's kind of a mess."

"Oh, that's not offensive at all," Matilda said, then forced him back into the choke hold.

"Your cheerleading coach will teach you the routines and make you look the part. She's got a lot of experience," Brand said. "Mindy?"

A door opened, and a gorgeous platinum-haired girl in a black bodysuit stepped into the room. Her legs had knives strapped to them and her belt was lined with razor-sharp throwing stars.

"Brand, if you call me Mindy one more time, I'm going to give you a makeover with my boot. The name is the Hyena."

END TRANSMISSION.

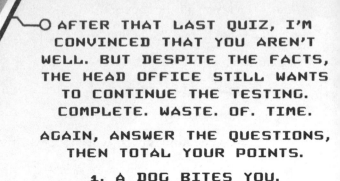

AFTER THAT LAST QUIZ, I'M CONVINCED THAT YOU AREN'T WELL. BUT DESPITE THE FACTS, THE HEAD OFFICE STILL WANTS TO CONTINUE THE TESTING. COMPLETE. WASTE. OF. TIME.

AGAIN, ANSWER THE QUESTIONS, THEN TOTAL YOUR POINTS.

1. A DOG BITES YOU.
WHAT DO YOU DO?

a. RUN CRYING TO THE HOSPITAL (4 POINTS)
b. ENJOY THE BEAUTIFUL PAIN AND THANK THE DOG (9 POINTS)
c. TRACK THE DOG BACK TO ITS FAMILY AND EXACT REVENGE ON ALL OF THEM (9 POINTS)
d. BITE THE DOG BACK (10 POINTS)

2. A STRANGER SMILES AT YOU. WHAT DO YOU DO?

a. RUN TO YOUR SECRET PLACE WHERE NO ONE CAN SEE YOU (7 POINTS)
b. SMILE BACK (1 POINT)
c. SHAKE YOUR FISTS AND CHASE HIM THROUGH THE STREETS (9 POINTS)

d. REMIND HIM THAT BARING HIS TEETH IS A SIGN OF AGGRESSION IN THE ANIMAL KINGDOM—THEN ATTACK! (10 POINTS)

3. WHAT DO YOU LIKE TO WATCH ON TV?

a. DOCUMENTARIES ABOUT RUTHLESS DICTATORS (7 POINTS)

b. STATIC (7 POINTS)

c. I DON'T OWN A TV. "THEY" CAN SEE ME THROUGH IT. (10 POINTS)

d. I HAD A TV. I HIT IT WITH A BAT. NOW IT DOESN'T WORK. (10 POINTS)

4. IF YOU HAD A BILLION DOLLARS, WHAT WOULD YOU SPEND IT ON?

a. DEATH RAY (10 POINTS)

b. SECRET FORTRESS (5 POINTS)

c. ARMY OF GOONS (7 POINTS)

d. ARMY OF UNICORNS WITH HORNS THAT SHOOT FIRE (1 POINT—WHO WOULDN'T WANT AN ARMY OF UNICORNS WITH HORNS THAT SHOOT FIRE?)

5. CONFESS SOMETHING THAT NO ONE KNOWS ABOUT YOU.

a. I ATTEND A SCHOOL FOR WIZARDS (10 POINTS)

b. I DATE A VAMPIRE (10 POINTS)

c. I'M THE CHILD OF A GREEK GOD (10 POINTS)

d. I'M A DETECTIVE WHO INVESTIGATES CRIMES COMMITTED BY FAIRY-TALE CHARACTERS (10 POINTS)

OK, LETS SEE THAT NUMBER.

_____

GREAT GOOGLY-MOOGLY! I DIDN'T KNOW NUMBERS WENT THAT HIGH! EXCUSE ME WHILE I BACK AWAY FROM YOU . . . SLOWLY.

7

The Hyena dashed into the hall-
way, heart racing, and slammed the door behind her.

"I told you it wasn't safe to go in there unarmed," Jackson said.

The Hyena gingerly touched the red welt around her eye. "No one told me she was such a pit bull. I fought a rabid tiger with a Wiffle ball bat once, but it was a kitten compared to her."

"Wheezer's not happy about this mission," Duncan said.

There was a terrible crash from behind the training room door.

"Well, she needs to grow up. She's a secret agent and this is her job. What's the big deal about a little exfoliating and a hot-oil treatment?"

"No one wants to hear that they could be pretty if they just tried. It's insulting," Ruby explained.

"Listen, her hair looks like a Swiffer sheet in need of a change. Her skin is sandpaper. She's got one eyebrow, and her clothes look like a pile of dirty laundry."

"Wheezer looks like that because she wants to," Flinch said.

"Yeah, she likes being different," Jackson said. "Cheerleaders tend to look alike. Turning her into one is her worst nightmare."

"It doesn't help that the person doing the makeover is a former beauty queen, either," Duncan added.

"I don't know what you guys think I do all day, but I'm a pretty busy secret agent. I got yanked out of the middle of a mission to do this, and I've got to get back within twenty-four hours or risk blowing my cover, putting a lot of my team in danger. So let's make a few things clear. I'm not here to judge her. If her inner beauty makes her a supermodel, well, zip-a-dee-doo-dah. But in my experience, cheerleaders tend to have a lot of outer beauty. If she wants this mission to succeed, she needs to be pretty, and I'm going to make her that way if I have to knock her out and moisturize her stupid, unconscious face."

"What can we do to help?" Ruby asked.

"Have the paramedics on standby," the Hyena said as she did a few stretches then ran in place to warm up. When she felt ready, she reached into her pocket and pulled out a set of tweezers. "I'm going back in."

"Keep an eye on her teeth," Flinch warned. "She bites."

"We've all learned that the hard way," Duncan said.

The Hyena took a deep breath and then opened the door.

"I will never forget you," Jackson said just as it slammed shut.

The Hyena stepped into complete darkness. Matilda had broken all the lightbulbs in the room. Smart move. If she couldn't be seen, she couldn't be tweezed. Plus, it gave her a combat edge since her eyes had more time to adjust to the low light. Still, as a highly trained former would-be assassin and current spy, the Hyena had learned a few things about finding people who preferred to stay hidden.

"Wheezer, we can do this the easy way or we can do it the hard way. Either way, I'm turning you into a babe."

"Bring it on, you beauty pageant has-been," Wheezer's voice said from the shadows.

The Hyena bristled. Has-been? She was Oklahoma's Tornado Alley Twister Princess two years in a row! She had been first runner-up in the Ms. Tweenager Pageant! She had retired at the top of her game!

"There's no need to get personal," she said, but her words were drowned out by the sound of rocket engines. Suddenly, the room lit up like a fireworks display. Temporarily blinded, the Hyena did not see Wheezer fly over her head, but she felt the kick in the ear. Instinctively, the Hyena leaped out of Wheezer's path, slamming into a wall. Her ear and her shoulder burned.

"Count your lucky stars, Secret Agent Barbie," Matilda shouted as she circled back for another attack. "I could have taken your head off your shoulders."

As Matilda boasted, the Hyena studied her for weaknesses. She could see two: anger influenced her decisions, and she left her feet exposed when she flew. The Hyena planned to use them both against her. "You're pretty confident for a girl who needs a stepping stool to get onto the toilet."

Wheezer snarled and made a beeline for her.

The Hyena had to time her attack just right. If she missed by even the slightest margin, there was a good chance Matilda would give her another black eye. So she locked eyes with Wheezer, and just before impact, she leaned backward like a sapling in the wind and snatched Wheezer by the sneakers.

"Gotcha!" the Hyena cried in triumph, holding on to Wheezer's foot as she sailed around the room. "That's a little trick I learned in gymnastics—something I used in my highly successful career as a beauty pageant contestant and now as a highly successful spy."

She hoped she sounded confident, because she was sure she was going to die. Matilda kicked and bounced around the room in an effort to lose her unwanted passenger. The Hyena was rolled and shaken, dipped and dragged. Somehow she found the strength to climb up Wheezer's body one inch at a time until she was sitting on her back.

"Set us down!" she demanded.

"No!!!"

"Stop being a baby!" the Hyena said. "It's not going to hurt . . . that much."

"I'm not being a baby! I don't want to be beautiful."

The Hyena knew it was time to do something drastic. She clamped one hand over Wheezer's eyes. Matilda lost control and the two buzzed around the room as blind as bats. With Matilda vulnerable, the Hyena reached around with her tweezers, grasped a rather thick follicle from between Matilda's eyes, and yanked. Wheezer bellowed like a branded bull, and the two fell to the hard floor.

The Hyena had no time to nurse her wounds. She jumped on top of Wheezer and pinned Wheezer's arms down with her knees. Then the plucking really began.

"Owww!" Matilda cried. "That hurt!"

"Stop complaining. You'll get used to it."

"I don't want to get used to it. I like my eyebrows the way they are," Wheezer said.

"Eyebrows is the plural of eyebrow, but you have one giant one! You can't be a cheerleader if you look like Bert from *Sesame Street*. Now hold still," the Hyena said.

Matilda frowned. "I *want* to look like this!"

"Listen, when this mission is over, you can go back to being a hairy freak, but right now you have to save the world. And to do that, you have to be hot," the Hyena said, yanking on another stray hair.

"Owww!" Wheezer screamed.

Twenty minutes later Matilda's one eyebrow was two. When the Hyena handed her a mirror to show her the results, Matilda was so exhausted from fighting that she barely registered the change. "Am I done?"

"Done? Kid, we've barely begun!"

The next seven hours were the most grueling of the Hyena's life. She dug deep into her encyclopedic knowledge of beauty secrets as well as her extensive background in restraining people. After she strapped Wheezer to a table, she went to work conditioning, shampooing, and detangling. She exfoliated with green teas, algae, and sand. She hosed the girl down with sunless tanners and wrapped her in eucalyptus leaves stuffed with mud and chocolate. She oversaw a laser teeth-whitening process, then covered the girl's face in avocado and cayenne pepper. Wheezer's toenails nearly required a belt sander to polish and trim. She was dunked repeatedly into a vat of moisturizer to combat her scaly feet and arms. By the time she was finished, the Hyena was covered in scratches and bruises, a clump of her hair was missing, and one of her front teeth was loose. But Matilda Choi was beautiful from head to toe.

The next morning at eight o'clock the Hyena limped into

Nathan Hale's gymnasium. She carried a boom box and was wearing black dancing apparel. Matilda was waiting, but she was wearing a shirt that looked as if she had stolen it from the world's fattest man.

"What are you wearing?"

"I'm comfortable." Matilda scowled.

"You look like you're trapped in a parachute. You can't wear that to learn how to cheer. Your arms and legs need to be loose and free."

"They're free enough to knock you out," Matilda threatened.

The two girls stared at one another for a long moment, sizing up who would win in a fistfight. The Hyena had to admit she wasn't sure. "Fine!" she cried. "Wear what you want! We'll start with some basic stuff—clapping."

"I don't need a lesson on how to clap."

"Oh yeah? Let's see."

The Hyena watched Matilda clap her hands like she had just seen a great movie. It was lazy and erratic. "Ta-da! Next lesson."

"That's nice if you're cheering on a tractor pull, but that's not a cheerleading clap. First of all, you have to hold your hands at chin level. Your fingers need to be tight and your hands like blades. You don't spread your arms farther apart than your shoulders. It's very specific."

Matilda tried it grudgingly. She had the same reaction to everything the Hyena had her do. Wheezer could perform flawless handsprings and backflips, and jump and kick like the best cheerleader ever. But cheerleading requires enthusiasm and a smile, and Matilda didn't have either. She mumbled a few cheers. Her smile looked like a grimace. Her body language screamed disgust and disdain. After hours of fruitless effort the Hyena threw up her hands. "This is pointless!" she declared.

"Exactly!" Matilda said.

"Cheerleaders have a lot of pep and enthusiasm. You act like you're at a funeral."

Matilda snarled. "I'm doing the best I can!"

"No, you're not," the Hyena barked. "You have a lousy attitude. Do you think the National Cheerleading Association is looking for a girl who wipes her nose with her pom-poms? You may think you're too good for this, but there are a thousand girls out there who really want to be cheerleaders and you're taking their spot! You can't even give them the respect of doing a good job."

Matilda stomped her foot. "It's no secret around here that I'm not a girlie-girl. I want a break."

"A break? The tryouts are tomorrow, Wheezer! I'm trying to teach you something that takes months to learn, and you only have tonight to learn it. We don't have time for a break or your bad attitude."

The Hyena wanted to clobber Wheezer—really, just kick her in the backside with her boot—but what would it solve? Nothing! She was wasting her time. The NERDS would have to find Gerdie Baker some other way. The Hyena stomped across the gymnasium floor and out into the hall. There she punched a locker and growled.

"You're approaching her the wrong way," Duncan said. He was standing in the doorway and had clearly seen the whole thing.

"Oh yeah? How would you do it, sticky?"

"I'd stop trying to get her to adapt to your teaching and start adapting to her way of learning," Duncan said. "She's not like a lot of girls. She's interested in things most girls turn their noses up at. Find a way to connect to those things."

"So stop everything and get to know her? We don't have time."

Duncan nodded. "OK, then here are Matilda's five favorite things in order: professional wrestling, Ultimate Fighting, punching people in the face, punching people in the belly, kicking people."

"Cheerleading is not a combat sport!" the Hyena said.

"Isn't it? There's a lot of kicking and punching the air," Duncan said, then he turned and walked back down the hallway.

The Hyena watched the chubby boy waddle away and

thought about what he had said. Cheering and wrestling were so totally different. She looked up at the clock and sighed. They were running out of time, and she had run out of ideas. She might as well give it a try.

She pushed open the gymnasium doors and stepped inside. Matilda was lying in the center of the basketball court staring up at the ceiling. "Back for more?"

The Hyena stood over the girl. She stared down at her for a long time, trying to find the connection that Duncan spoke of—but cheerleading was all kicking and jumping and acrobatics, and wrestling was all . . .

"Let's try the clap one more time," the Hyena said.

Matilda got to her feet and rolled her eyes. She put her hands in position but without any excitement.

"I want you to imagine that there is a bad guy's head between your hands."

"Huh?"

"You're going to box his ears, which will mess up his balance and make him cry," the Hyena explained. "You don't want him to get away, so you have to keep your hands within your shoulders."

"That's good advice," Matilda said, her eyes suddenly sparkling.

"Plus, you keep your hands straight and tight. A quick and hard clap could burst his eardrums, which is a plus."

"Like this?" Matilda asked, suddenly producing a perfect cheerleading clap.

The Hyena smiled. "Exactly. It's very dark and troubling, but it's perfect. Now let's try some high kicks."

Matilda frowned.

"You know, like kicking someone in the face."

Matilda smiled.

The two girls went to work. The Hyena taught the tiny spy everything she knew, tailored to Matilda's violent hobbies. When Matilda imagined she was crushing someone's head using the T Stunt or corkscrew backflip, she did it with zeal.

They worked all through the night, and when the sun came up, the Hyena smiled. Matilda was a first-rate cheerleader, even with the bloodlust in her eyes.

The Hyena walked out of the gymnasium and found Agent Brand standing in the hallway.

"My work here is done," she said.

8

"Cheerleading?" Molly said skeptically.

"Cheerleading?" Matilda's brothers cried in unison.

"Cheerleading?" Ben said. "You want to be a cheerleader?"

Matilda nodded.

Mickey laughed. "That's hilarious!"

The other boys laughed uproariously. Marky fell off the sofa and groaned between giggles.

"Shut up, monkeys," Molly snapped, then turned her attention back to Ms. Holiday.

"My daughter wants to stand in front of football teams and wave pom-poms?" Molly asked. Her face was like stone.

"Um, yes," Ms. Holiday said. The librarian had come to the

Chois to convince Matilda's parents to allow her to try out for the NCA. Ben Choi seemed thrilled—and slightly bewildered by his daughter's new look. Molly, however, was intense and suspicious. She had totally stolen Ms. Holiday's confidence. Lisa felt as if the woman could hear her thoughts. "Just to be clear, competitive cheerleaders don't cheer for athletic teams. It's a sport unto itself, combining cheering with acrobatics and dance."

Ben spoke up, nodding. "Molly, cheering is very popular. I took some photographs of it for a magazine. People love it."

"That makes no sense," Marky said. "If there is no team, who are they cheering for?"

"Marky, hush!" Molly scolded, then turned back to Ms. Holiday. "That makes no sense."

Ms. Holiday turned to Wheezer, who sat on a couch nearby. She hoped the girl might help win over her mother, but Wheezer just shrugged.

"If she makes the squad, she will go to a cheerleading camp right here in Arlington, where she and other girls her age will prepare for the national competition held on the Mall in D.C. She will be gone for a week, and completely supervised the whole time."

"Why does the school care about cheering in the summertime?" Molly said.

Ms. Holiday blinked. She wasn't prepared for such a question, even though it was perfectly reasonable. Of course the school didn't care about cheerleading! What could she say? Mrs. Choi looked as if she could smell a lie from a thousand miles away.

"They think it will help me come out of my shell," Matilda said.

"I've seen you come out of your shell. Tell them you should go back in," Moses said. This made the other boys fall all over themselves once again.

Molly stood up. "All of you. Go bounce an egg! Out!" she bellowed.

The boys ran out of the room like they were trying to escape from an erupting volcano. When they were gone, Molly returned to her seat. Her eyes locked on to Ms. Holiday's once more. The librarian could feel the suspicion radiating off her.

"It will also teach me some leadership qualities," Matilda said.

"Leadership?"

"Sure!" Ms. Holiday said. "It will teach her how to work in a team."

Molly rolled her eyes. "Matilda does not need to know how to work in a team. She needs to know how to lead one. She comes from a family of very strong women. Her brothers will need her guidance. You saw them! What can silly cheerleading give my daughter to make her brothers fear her?"

Ms. Holiday stood up from her chair and straightened her skirt. She couldn't let this woman get in the way of the security of the world.

"I was a cheerleader when I was in college, Mrs. Choi. In fact, the only reason I went to college was because I won a cheerleading scholarship. When I got there, the other girls pushed me around. But I worked hard, and before any of them knew it I was the captain of the squad, and I made *them* work hard. Most of the girls learned to respect me and the ones who didn't learned to fear me. When it was all said and done, my squad won the national championship. You want to know how many disorganized, disrespectful girls I had to manage, Mrs. Choi? Twenty-four! If you let Matilda try out for this team, I think the things she'll learn about leadership will be more than enough to handle six rowdy brothers. Much more than enough!"

"Ben?" Molly asked.

Mr. Choi smiled. "I'm all for it. Anything that gets Matilda out of those ragamuffin clothes and combat boots she likes so much. Look at her. What a beauty! I say yes."

Molly's eyes narrowed and a disapproving crease appeared in between her brows. She shook her head, then stood up and left the room.

"I'm sorry, Ms. Holiday," Ben said as he got up from his chair. "Matilda's mother and I rarely see eye to eye these days, but I have to respect her choices even if I don't agree."

Ms. Holiday watched as Mr. Choi followed Molly out of the room. "Alexander is going to roar. It drives him nuts that he needs a parent's permission to send an agent out to save the world."

"Maybe the Hyena can go in my place," Matilda said, trying not to look too happy.

Just then, Molly returned with something under her arm. "You cannot go, Little M, unless someone from our family goes along to look after you." She offered Matilda the little stone statue from her room. "Take old grandfather with you. Keep him in your pocket. He will protect you whether you are cheerleading"—she turned her eyes to the librarian—"or doing something dangerous."

Ms. Holiday swallowed hard.

9

Matilda and Agent Brand sat outside the YMCA in Arlington, Virginia. A steady stream of pretty girls stepped through a set of double doors for the tryouts for Team Strikeforce, the elite Junior East Coast Division cheerleading squad that the NERDS believed Gerdie had joined. A thousand girls like Matilda had come from all over the country for what was rumored to be nine vacant spots. Unlike Matilda, they were full of pep and smiles. She wanted to punch them all in the face. She hated her skirt flapping on her legs. She hated the hour it had taken to do her hair and makeup. She hated the pains in her cheeks from smiling. If she was going undercover, it should have been as a bullfighter or a *luchador*! It didn't help that these girls went through the doors to the auditorium happy

and high-spirited, only to come out sobbing into their hands. It made Matilda nervous. Not about failing or even looking foolish—she sort of expected that. No, she was worried about feeding one of her fists to the judges. Whatever they were saying to the hopefuls was brutal. She hadn't seen so much blubbering since the time she challenged the men of the Alpha Sigma Phi fraternity to a punch fight.

Mr. Brand seemed even more nervous than Matilda. Most of the time the former spy was unflappable. Matilda had heard he once fought off a dozen assassins with only his fists and a bottle of champagne. But today he kept tapping the heel of his right shoe on the marble floor like a jackhammer. Perhaps he was just uncomfortable out of his tuxedo. Today, to keep a low profile, he was dressed in linen pants and a white shirt.

"Why isn't the Hyena here to give me pointers?" Matilda said, hoping to distract the spy from his tapping. "You weren't a cheerleader, were you?"

Mr. Brand shook his head. "The Hyena has other responsibilities."

"Yeah? What are those, exactly?"

Brand stiffened. "Sorry, but you don't have security clearance for that kind of information."

Wheezer was stunned. "I have the highest security clearance in the country. I have higher security clearance than the president!"

Brand's face told her not to press the issue. The Hyena's mission was a secret for another day.

"Ms. Holiday cheered in college. Why didn't she come?"

"Ms. Holiday was transferred to the team just days before the Mathlete's mom moved them to Ohio. They spent very little time together, but if Gerdie were to recognize Lisa, our plan would fail," Brand said.

"Oh, she's Lisa, now?"

Brand blushed. "Ms. Holiday and I have become . . . friends."

"Friends that kiss and hug?"

Matilda could tell the man was uncomfortable. He kept tugging at his collar as if it were strangling him.

"Ms. Holiday sent along a list of tips and a cookie," he said, shoving them into her hands.

Matilda quickly put the cookie aside. Ms. Holiday was a wonderful lady, but her baking bordered on dangerous. The cookie was as hard as a manhole cover. She opened the letter. "'Dear Matilda, Here is my best advice for your tryout. First, you have to be positive. No one wants to see a grouchy cheerleader.'"

"She told me to practice smiling with you," Brand said. "Flash me your best smile."

Matilda smiled.

Agent Brand cringed.

"What?"

"You're supposed to look happy when you smile."

"Well, give me something to smile about."

"Think about ponies. Girls love ponies, right?"

Matilda frowned. "I don't."

"Ribbons?"

"Uh-uh."

"Doll babies?"

"I'm almost twelve!"

"Then what do you like?"

"Hmm . . . demolitions, explosions, bonfires," Matilda said. "I like to watch barroom brawls. I love sports that involve an ax and pretty much anything to do with pro wrestling!"

"I see," Brand said. "Imagine you and one of these pro wrestlers went to the park. What a beautiful day it is. The sun is shining. There isn't a cloud in the—"

"And we found some bullies and gave them all head butts! While they were dazed, I climbed up in a tree and leaped onto their heads for a superatomic dog. Then, when they were down, we smashed a steel chair across their backs!"

"Why was there a steel chair in the park?" Brand asked. Then he sighed. "It doesn't matter. What's important is that you are smiling, but you might want to work on it. I suspect they don't want a cheerleader who looks like she's an escaped mental patient."

Matilda glared and then returned to Ms. Holiday's list. "'Second, make eye contact with the judges. They want to feel like you are cheering right to them.'"

"Eye contact, right," Brand said. "Remember what we taught you in your spy training. Looking someone in the eye can elicit a sense of trust and welcoming."

"Really? 'Cause I've been using it to intimidate people. You should see how it works on dogs! They run off like they've seen the devil."

"Keep reading."

"'The third thing is play up your strengths,'" Matilda read. "What are my strengths?"

She could tell Brand wasn't comfortable with giving compliments. "You are a gifted athlete. Use your acrobatic skills. Also, try to turn some of that happy energy you have when you knock out someone's teeth into a positive expression of hope and joy. If that doesn't help, I had the brains at the Playground build you something."

He pulled a briefcase from beneath their seat. Inside were four brand-new asthma inhalers and a leather belt with tiny slots to hold them.

"What are these?" Matilda asked, gazing at them with wonder.

"Specialty inhalers."

Matilda strapped the belt around her waist. "And a utility belt! I'm like an asthmatic Batman!"

"These might come in handy on this mission. The blue set acts as an underwater breathing apparatus. There's enough concentrated air in them to keep you alive for six hours. You never know when something like that might come in handy. The green set is what we hope will help you today. One squeeze of the plunger and it'll lift you off the ground."

"Um . . . I have a set that does that already."

"Not like these. These are stealth inhalers. No explosions. No rocket flames. They're whisper-quiet. You will be able to jump, backflip, and somersault higher than any of the other girls. Gluestick says that a long pump could allow you to reach the observation platform of the Empire State Building, not that you'll need that today."

"Very cool, but it does feel like we're cheating, Mr. Brand," Matilda said.

"All is fair in love and national security. What else is in the letter?"

Matilda turned her attention back to Ms. Holiday's notes. "It says, 'No wooing'?"

"Lisa—I mean, Ms. Holiday—says it's sort of a nervous reaction some girls do when they are out on the floor. They start 'wooing.'"

"That's silly. I can promise you that I will not 'woo'!"

"See that you don't. She says it's very annoying."

The door opened and a pretty red-haired girl poked her head out into the hall. Her face was one big smile and her eyes were bright with excitement. She reminded Matilda of Flinch the time he ate three Cookiepuss ice cream cakes in one sitting. They couldn't get him off the ceiling for an hour. "Matilda Choi? Are you ready to BRING IT?"

Matilda nodded and stood up. She turned to Agent Brand. "Well, I guess I have to go 'bring it' now."

"How about one more attempt at a smile?" the spy said.

Matilda forced one on to her face. "How is this?"

"You look like you've just been stung by a wasp," Mr. Brand said. "It looked better when you were daydreaming about braining someone. Think steel chairs!"

Matilda walked through the door into the darkly lit gymnasium. In the center of the room was a spotlight and beyond that a stage where seven shadowy figures sat at a table. When she stepped into the spotlight, she was unable to see her judges at all. It was probably just as well. If she had to look at seven more grinning idiots, she might never get through her audition. The only drawback was that she couldn't start searching for Gerdie Baker. If she caught Mathlete right away, she could avoid the whole mission entirely. It had only been a couple days, but she was growing weary of exfoliating her pores.

"Name!" a girl shouted.

"Matilda Choi."

"Matilda is not a good name for a cheerleader. We'll call you Maddie."

The rest of the girls murmured in agreement, then turned their attention back to Matilda.

"OK, Maddie, cheer for us. And try not to waste our time," a voice demanded.

Matilda nodded and took a quick shot of her medicinal inhaler.

"Today!" another judge snapped.

Ironically, it was her judges who provided Matilda with a smile, courtesy of a daydream in which she kicked them all in the face. "Ready? OK!" she shouted, and then she clapped her hands, imagining slamming a judge's head. "We've got spirit. Yes we do! We've got spirit. How about you?"

She did three backflips and a back handspring before running forward into a one-handed cartwheel. She then flipped end over end three times before landing perfectly on her feet. Each time she jumped she used her new inhalers for an extra couple of feet of lift. On her next run, two more super front-end handsprings became a complete one-hundred-and-eighty-degree flip, a jump she could never have done on her own. She ended her routine in a perfect split.

She sat with her hands on her hips, grinning as best she could and staring up at her seven shadowed judges. Were they impressed? They just sat there without a word. They could probably tell she was a fake—the cheers, makeup, and clothes weren't fooling anyone! She had failed the mission.

Then her mouth opened and she did something she thought she would never do.

"Woooooooooooooooo!"

"You're in, Choi," one of the judges said. "Welcome to Team Strikeforce."

"What? Really?" Matilda couldn't believe how happy she felt. In fact, it made her angry that she could get so much pleasure from being accepted by these strangers. If she hadn't been on a mission, she would have been more than thrilled to tell them where they could shove their acceptance. But she nodded, thanked the judges, and left the gymnasium without punching a single person.

Mr. Brand was waiting outside the door where she had left him. He looked fidgety, cracking his knuckles and tapping his foot. "What happened? I heard wooing!"

END TRANSMISSION.

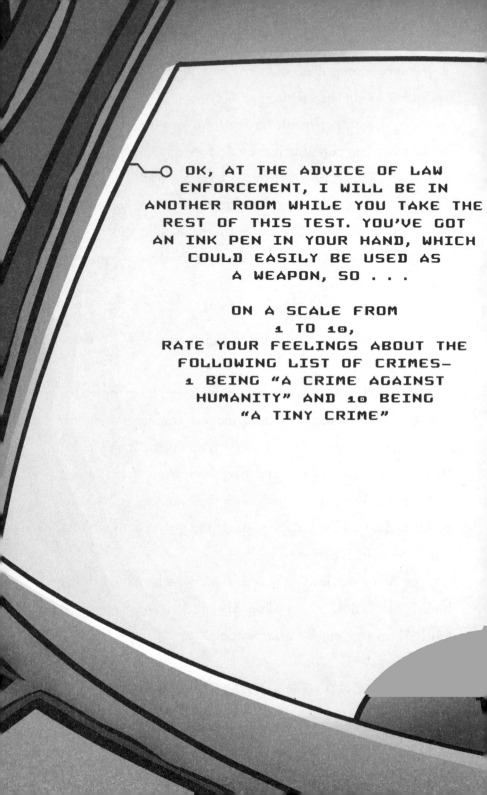

OK, AT THE ADVICE OF LAW ENFORCEMENT, I WILL BE IN ANOTHER ROOM WHILE YOU TAKE THE REST OF THIS TEST. YOU'VE GOT AN INK PEN IN YOUR HAND, WHICH COULD EASILY BE USED AS A WEAPON, SO . . .

ON A SCALE FROM 1 TO 10, RATE YOUR FEELINGS ABOUT THE FOLLOWING LIST OF CRIMES— 1 BEING "A CRIME AGAINST HUMANITY" AND 10 BEING "A TINY CRIME"

1. DRIVING A CAR INTO AN
   ORPHANAGE
   —

2. TAKING THE WORLD HOSTAGE
   —

3. KIDNAPPING SOMEONE'S PET
   —

4. TOPPLING A GOVERNMENT
   —

5. CREATING HUMAN/ANIMAL HYBRIDS
   BENT ON WORLD DOMINATION
   —

6. BETRAYING THE HUMAN RACE TO
   ALIEN OVERLORDS
   —

7. TRYING TO OPEN A DIMENSIONAL
   DOOR TO A DEMON DIMENSION
   —

8. BUILDING A GIANT ROBOT TO
   CRUSH THE CITY
   —

9. BLOWING UP THE MOON
   —

10. MAKING YOUR MOTHER CRY
    —

11. LAUGHING WHILE YOUR MOTHER CRIES
    —

OK, LET'S TALLY THOSE NUMBERS.

IT'S TROUBLING HOW HIGH THIS NUMBER
IS. ALL OF THESE CRIMES ARE REALLY,
REALLY BAD.

YOU ARE A SICK LITTLE MONKEY.

ACCESS GRANTED

BEGIN TRANSMISSION:

10

Heathcliff—or rather, Choppers, I mean, Simon . . . no, Screwball, or whatever his name was— hated the Arlington Hospital for the Criminally Insane. He hated the doctors and the nurses. He hated the security guards. He hated the dull gray paint on every wall and the bland meals served with plastic utensils. He hated the dingy fluorescent lights and the patch of dying grass they called the yard. He swore to himself that when he ruled the world the first thing he would do was destroy the hospital—with a big wrecking ball, or maybe explosives—no, a rocket! In fact, imagining the building in flames helped him pass the endless hours with a smile on his face.

But there was one thing he thoroughly enjoyed about being

locked up in the loony bin: arts and crafts class. Twice a week the patients were herded into the art room and encouraged to explore their feelings using clay, paint, papier-mâché, and ribbons. On this day, Screwball was working with glue, dried corn, peas, and other vegetables. It was then that he discovered a new passion. If the whole "taking over the world" thing didn't pan out, he might have a lucrative career as a street artist.

"OK, everyone," Dr. Sontag said. "I'm happy to see so many of you working on your projects with so much focus. It's time to share what you have created. Why don't we start with Bob?"

Heathcliff sneered. Bob was a serial kidnapper. He also had no eye for color or line. When the stumbling fool raised his canvas, it took all of Screwball's self-control not to rip it into shreds and laugh in the stupid man's face. A rowboat on a little river? That's what Bob called art?

"A lovely day on the water," Dr. Sontag said. "Why don't you tell us how this makes you feel?"

"My dad used to take me to this river when I was little— before I started to hear the voices," Bob blubbered.

Screwball rolled his eyes.

"It looks like it meant a lot to you, Bob. Let's move on to Chucky," the doctor said. "Let's see your masterpiece."

Chucky Swiller was a slack-jawed idiot with a face like an

orangutan. He also had the artistic talent of one. Paint was everywhere—and mostly on his dopey freckled face.

"I made a house," Chucky said.

"And it's on fire," Dr. Sontag said with a little worried frown on her face. Chucky was in the hospital because he liked to play with matches and gasoline.

"Oh, is that what you made?" Screwball said. "'Cause what it looks like is you drank your paints then barfed them all over the canvas!"

Dr. Sontag frowned. "Heathcliff! This is not a place of judgment. However Chucky chooses to create his art is valid. Apologize to him!"

Screwball sighed. "Chucky, I'm sorry. Sorry that you are clearly colorblind and don't know the first thing about perspective or three-dimensional drafting. I'm sorry your work is bad, but mostly I feel sorry for me, as I'm the only one who cares enough about you to tell you that you are terrible and should stop painting. You should go back to being a pyromaniac and stop victimizing the world with your art."

Dr. Sontag's face puckered with impatience. She took a deep breath and appeared to be mouthing numbers to calm herself. When she finished, she turned to Screwball.

"OK, Heathcliff. Show us what you have made."

"Dr. Sontag, I have asked you to call me Screwball."

Sontag sighed with exhaustion. "Screwball, show us what you created."

Screwball held his work out proudly. It was a triptych—a three-paneled painting—featuring images of great destruction made from dried vegetables. The panel on the left showed little snow-pea people running and screaming as a giant turnip robot stomped down the street after them. The panel on the right featured a sea of green-bean prisoners marching across a field of flames with armed guards eyeing their every step. In the center panel there was a baby carrot and pearl onion depiction of Heathcliff himself, sitting upon a gigantic throne that was crushing planet Earth.

Dr. Sontag sighed again. "Everyone, how does this make you feel?"

Dr. Trouble slowly raised his hand and Dr. Sontag called on him. "Yes, Dr. Trouble? Does Heathcliff . . . I mean, Screwball's work make you feel anything?"

"Sad . . . scared."

"It made me wet my pants," Chucky said.

Screwball smiled proudly. "See, Chucky, good art creates emotional responses in the audience. I wanted you to wet yourself and you did! And now I'd like to tell you how it makes me feel. This work is important because it is more than a piece made from dried produce; it's a glimpse of your unavoidable future. You'll notice I used lentils to indicate despair on the faces of my victims. And my self-portrait looks good enough to eat. Bow before my artistic genius!"

"Everyone, I think we can call it a day," Dr. Sontag said. "I need to talk to my boss about being reassigned, anyway."

The doors to the room opened and several huge guards entered. Screwball ignored them and carefully set aside his masterpiece. Peas and carrots were very delicate and he wanted to preserve the triptych. Someday, when he was running things, the masses would want to see his early work as an artist.

"*Pssss*," he heard. Screwball turned to one of the guards and snarled. Then he realized the man was not another one of the muscle-bound fools that tormented him daily but, instead, his very own goon!

"Old friend! How did you get in here?" he whispered back.

"I knocked out the guard and took his uniform. He's sleeping in the Dumpster, safe and sound. I wanted to give you an update. Mathlete has built her machine. She's opening rifts everywhere she goes."

"Are there side effects?" Heathcliff said.

The goon nodded. "The government is trying to keep it quiet, but an alligator as big as a dump truck was captured in Topeka, Kansas. Plus they're missing a few cement mixers in Minneapolis and an entire library disappeared in St. Louis."

"That's excellent news," Screwball said.

"Even better news," the goon said. "I can get you out of here."

"No need, my friend," Screwball said.

The goon was visibly surprised. "Have they finally made you lose your mind? Why do you want to stay?"

"Because it will be so much more satisfying when my bitterest enemies come and release me! They will have no choice but to unlock the doors and let me out."

"Your enemies?"

Screwball nodded, then practiced his evil laugh. "Yes, NERDS will be pounding on the door of this hospital to free me before you know it."

SUPPLEMENTAL MATERIAL

The following "art" was seized from Heathcliff Hodges's room at the Arlington Hospital for the Criminally Insane. Despite his efforts, neither the Smithsonian, the Metropolitan Museum of Art in New York, nor the Louvre in Paris, France, expressed interest in an exhibition.

11

Matilda hefted her duffel bag and climbed aboard the bus to cheerleading camp. Inside, she faced a gang of dazzlingly pretty girls with the most sour, pouty looks she had ever seen. They eyed her up and down the way someone might look at a public toilet.

"Hold it right there," one girl said. She was blonde and blue-eyed and would have been pretty if not for her expression of disgust. "Don't think that just 'cause you're on Team Strikeforce that you are *on* Team Strikeforce. You're not actually one of us until I say you are, and right now I'm saying you're not."

"Yeah," the others chimed.

Matilda laughed. She knew these girls, or at least their type. They were bullies. Nathan Hale Elementary was full of them.

Luckily, after putting up with their torment for years, she knew exactly how to handle bullies.

"What's your name?"

"Tiffany," the blonde girl said, scowling.

"So, you're in charge, huh? I can tell by the way these brainless morons worship you."

The other girls bristled.

"That's not true at all!" a pretty redhead snapped as she texted furiously on her phone. "I'm so posting how rude you are!"

Tiffany flashed the redhead an ugly look. "Actually, that's exactly how it is! Shut up, McKenna!" She turned back to Matilda, but before she could say anything a horrible sneeze flew out of Matilda's nose.

"Wheezer, can you hear me?" Brand blared through Matilda's comlink. His voice was so loud it rattled her brain. She wished she could shut it off, but no amount of squeezing her nose could stop her shaking eardrums.

"Turn it down a notch!" she cried.

After a second she realized everyone on the bus was looking at her as if she had lost her mind. Tiffany laughed, and the others echoed her.

"She's already snapping under the pressure, girls!" Tiffany crowed. "I suggest you get off the bus and go home, 'cause it isn't going to get any easier."

"I'm staying," Matilda said.

"I am not sitting with the crazy girl," McKenna declared as the girls settled into the farthest reaches of the bus, leaving Matilda alone at the front.

"What do you want?" she mumbled.

Brand's voice crackled to life. "Wheezer, I've been waiting for a report. I thought you might be in trouble."

"A little busy being bullied by the other girls on the bus, boss," Matilda said. "None of them look like Gerdie Baker. If she's here, she's had a lot of plastic surgery. Listen, I'll check in when I get a moment to myself. There's not a lot of room on this bus."

"Understood," Brand said.

The bus pulled into a sprawling campground surrounded by acres and acres of dense woods. There was a pond with a dock, a half-dozen wooden cabins, a small administrative building, and a handful of picnic tables around a big green practice yard. When they got off the bus, Matilda and the girls met representatives of the NCA, much older but just as peppy as the rest of the cheerleaders. They assigned everyone a cabin and told the girls when to expect breakfast, lunch, and dinner. They also told the girls there were only two rules at the camp: one, don't wander around in the woods, and two, have a "cheer-tastic time."

Matilda circled until she found her cabin, but since she was the last one through the door, she was left with the worst bunk—a moth-eaten mattress with a paper-thin pillow.

Tiffany and McKenna sneered at her as she dumped her duffel bag on the bed.

"I can't believe they stuck her in here with us!" McKenna grumbled to Tiffany. Then they ran off, leaving Matilda alone.

Matilda shrugged it off and crammed her bag under her cot. Then she reached up to unfasten the lock on the window near her bed.

"Do yourself a favor and don't open that window. The portable toilets are right outside."

Matilda turned and found a girl standing in the doorway of the cabin. She was as pretty as the others, but something in her face gave her a kind expression.

"Ugh," Matilda said as she refastened the lock.

"I heard you got stuck in Tiffany's cabin. I thought it would be nice to come by and make sure you were still alive," the girl said, laughing.

"Next time you might want to check on *her*, not me," Matilda said.

"Don't let Tiffany bother you," the girl said. "She's been cheering since she was in diapers, or so she says. None of us really know each other that well, but somehow on the first day she became the boss. I've seen her type before. I think she likes it when you fight back."

Matilda nodded. "Then she's going to love my right hook."

"I'm Kylie," the girl said.

"I'm Matilda," she replied, remembering to practice her smile. Kylie gave one back, then offered to help her unpack. While they worked, she filled Matilda in on the other girls on the team: McKenna spent most of her day texting and updating her many online profiles; Pammy and Lilly were called "the makeup twins" and hogged every available mirror; the striking Asian girl with purple eye shadow was named Jeannie; the two African-American girls were Toni and Shauna. Including Matilda, there were nine more new girls, but Kylie hadn't had a chance to meet them yet. Matilda did the math. All in all, she had sixteen suspects, but she was relieved to be able to cut three from her list. Eliminating Jeannie, Toni, and Shauna would make things easier. No matter how much plastic surgery Gerdie might have gotten, she couldn't change her race. Still, that left thirteen girls.

Suddenly, McKenna returned to the cabin. "Hey, what are you two talking about?"

"You," Kylie said.

Matilda could almost smell McKenna's insecurity. It quickly turned to anger. "New roommates are losers!" she said as her fingers typed furiously on her phone. "Watch your step or I'll post something a lot worse next time."

The girls watched McKenna storm out of the cabin.

"Well, I guess we're not going to be friends with her," Kylie said with a laugh. "Anyway, it's dinnertime. They're serving meatloaf surprise. The surprise is that ten percent of the people who eat it actually survive."

"I'll catch up with you," Matilda said.

When Kylie was gone, Matilda fell onto her bunk and jotted down what she had learned about the rest of the squad into a notebook. Since the girls looked and dressed so much alike, she was going to have to work extra-hard to keep track of them.

She joined the other girls at dinner, studying each of their faces. She'd seen hundreds of photos of the old Gerdie, but none of these girls resembled her in the least. It was frustrating, but not nearly as much as their endless excited chatter about how they were going to "bring it" and "show those wannabes why Team Strikeforce is the best." Matilda feared she would leap onto the table and strangle one of them if they didn't shut up, so she excused herself to go back to her bunk and get some rest. Tiffany gave her a nasty smile as she stood up.

"Get your beauty sleep, loser," she said. "You need all you can get."

Exhausted, Matilda made a quick report to Agent Brand and fell sound asleep.

At five in the morning Matilda discovered exactly what Tiffany had meant about needing her sleep. She was shaken roughly and told to get into her practice uniform. She got dressed as quickly as possible and rushed out for what would be a twelve-hour ordeal.

Matilda did her best to keep up, but the practice was more grueling than her spy training, which often included barbed wire, an obstacle course, and robots shooting lasers at her. Learning the routines was simple enough, but Tiffany insisted on perfection. She wanted the squad to act like it was of one mind, with each clap, kick, and cheer performed at the exact same moment. Over the course of the day she cut two of the nine new cheerleaders they had chosen from Matilda's tryouts. The next day three more were gone. Shauna told Kylie and Matilda that Tiffany had accepted more girls than the team needed for the sole purpose of weeding them out.

"You mean I'm still trying out?" Matilda asked.

Kylie nodded. "Tiffany has already let McKenna, Pammy, Shauna, Toni, Lilly, Jeannie, and me know that we made the final squad."

"How many spots are left?" Matilda asked.

"One."

Matilda looked to the other three girls. It was important that she got that last spot.

When the second day of practice was over, she staggered into her cabin with complaining muscles and a head clogged with dance moves. She didn't even bother to eat, just climbed into her bunk and fell fast asleep. She planned to wake in the night and search the other girls' belongings for any clues that might point her to Gerdie, but exhaustion overwhelmed her. She slept until five a.m., only to be awoken to repeat the previous day.

Kylie smiled at her when they met on the practice field.

"Tiffany is the devil," Matilda groaned.

"Yes. Yes, she is," Kylie said.

"Quiet! Today we're going to learn a move called 'Shoot the Rocket,'" Tiffany said.

The girls gasped. Even the girls who'd already made the squad seemed shocked.

"What's the Rocket?" Matilda whispered to Kylie.

"It's an aerial stunt—very dangerous," she said. "Most high schools have banned it. Even pro cheerleaders get hurt doing it. It's superadvanced."

"Pyramid!" Tiffany barked, and Kylie and the other girls quickly assembled into a human pyramid, six bodies stacked on top of one another. Tiffany climbed to the top. She stood on McKenna and Pammy's backs and looked down at Matilda and the other three girls.

"Now listen up, 'cause I'm only saying this once. The Rocket is usually done with the help of a spotter who hoists the girl onto his hands at chest-level. Then you jump upward, do a corkscrew twirl, and land on your feet at the top of a pyramid. I say 'usually' because *we* do it differently." She grinned. "We cut out the spotter. Watch carefully."

Tiffany bent her knees and then leaped backward into the air. She did a corkscrew turn and then landed squarely on McKenna's and Pammy's backs. The girls let out a painful groan. Matilda could hardly believe what she had seen. It was an incredible move—like something only a highly trained secret agent might be able to do. *Could Tiffany be the Mathlete?*

"I think I'm going to be sick," one of the other new girls said. She and another of the new girls ran off the field and were never seen again. Matilda and one other girl were left for the last spot.

"Maddie, let's see what you can do," Tiffany said, climbing down off the pyramid to watch from the side.

"Just let me check my inhalers—I get a little asthmatic and—"

"No one cares about your stupid disease," McKenna said. "Are you going to do this stunt or not? I have text messages to respond to!"

Matilda climbed the pyramid slowly. When she got to the top, she could hardly stand up straight. It was clear McKenna and Pammy were trying to knock her off. She dug her shoes into their backs and they yelped in pain. Matilda smiled sheepishly at them and bent her knees. Leaping backward as hard as she could, she tapped her stealth inhalers and blasted into the air with a whisper-quiet thrust. She did the corkscrew spin during the flip and landed cleanly, making extra sure to plant her feet on McKenna's and Pammy's heads.

There was silence. Tiffany looked stunned, and Matilda's sole remaining competition dropped her head and walked out.

McKenna turned to look up at Matilda angrily. "This isn't over," she said, then rocked hard. The human pyramid began to sway and buckle. Then it collapsed. If Matilda fell from that height, she'd hurt herself badly, so she fired the inhaler once more and up she went, spiraling and forward-flipping gracefully until she landed right in front of Tiffany. The team leader eyed her closely.

"Welcome to Team Strikeforce," Tiffany said, red-faced and angry.

Once the pile of cheerleaders untangled themselves, Kylie found Matilda. "That was awesome," Kylie whispered to Matilda.

"Thanks," Matilda whispered back as she watched Tiffany storm off the field. "But I'm worried it was a little too awesome."

When the girls finished practicing "Shoot the Rocket," they headed to the kitchen for some dinner. Matilda snatched a banana and a peanut butter sandwich then raced back to the silence of the cabin. She had only a few opportunities to be alone and check in with the NERDS team. Once she closed the door, she squeezed her nose to activate her comlink.

"Congratulations are in order, Wheezer," Mr. Brand said. "I hear you are an official member of the squad."

"Don't tease me. This is so silly."

"Well, the world appreciates your sacrifice. Do you have any suspects?"

"Maybe Tiffany. She's got moves a normal kid doesn't usually have," Matilda said. "Everyone seems to think she's been cheering since she was in diapers, but you know as well as I do how a backstory can be invented. I'm keeping an eye on her. If you could have someone activate the comlink around three in the morning to wake me up, I'll search her stuff. But I don't know where she would hide that machine. If it's as big as Gluestick thinks it is, there's no place for it in this cabin. I'll have to search the other buildings."

"Happy hunting," Brand said.

"Wheezer, out."

Before she knew it, she was fast asleep and having terrible dreams about monstrous pom-poms chasing her through the woods. She was pulled out of the nightmare by a rougher-than-usual shaking. She leaped out of bed and swung wildly, her secret-agent training taking over. Her fist connected with someone's mouth.

"What do you think you're doing?" Jeannie shouted when the lights came on.

It was then that Matilda noticed that Jeannie was on the floor, clutching her cheek. She frowned and helped the girl to her feet. "I'm sorry. I can get a little jumpy. Are you OK?"

"Nothing a surgeon can't fix," the girl said angrily. "It's time to suit up."

Matilda glanced out the window. It was still pitch-black out—too early for practice. "Now? It's the middle of the night."

"Less talk, more action," Lilly snapped.

Matilda slipped into her clothes and stepped out of the cabin and into the night.

The moon was high in the sky over the practice field. The squad headed straight across it to the woods, and Matilda followed.

"Listen up, Maddie," Tiffany said.

"It's Matilda."

"It's what I say it is!" she roared. When she calmed, she continued. "The squad wants to invite you to take part in a little job."

"What kind of job?"

"Not so much a job—more like a shopping trip," McKenna said.

"Shop Op!" Shauna and Toni said together, then gave each other a high five.

"Sounds . . . fun. You do realize it's the middle of the night? What store is even open?" Matilda asked.

"It's not a store and it's not really shopping," McKenna said.

"But there is going to be some shop*lifting*," Jeannie added.

"Shoplifting?" Matilda said. Kylie stood nearby. From her expression, she was as unhappy about the plan as Matilda.

Tiffany bristled. "Cheerleading is an expensive sport. The uniforms, meals—hey, do you think this camp is free? Team Strikeforce doesn't have sponsors and the prize money is peanuts. The competition fee for the finals alone is more than my allowance until the end of time."

"So we've found a way to pay for it," Lilly said.

"By stealing?" Matilda asked.

Everyone nodded.

Matilda had never stolen anything in her life, but she knew she had to play along. "No arguments here. I've lifted a few tubes of lipstick and a purse. Shouldn't be a problem."

"Well, listen to public enemy number one," Pammy said, laughing.

McKenna lifted her arm to reveal an odd-looking glove that wrapped around her hand, forearm, and elbow. It had buttons and little glass screens mounted near the wrist that flashed numbers and images. Matilda knew immediately what it was. Gerdie had given her gigantic machine its own makeover.

"Are we far enough away from the camp?" Pammy asked. "That machine sucks all the energy out of everything. If we go back to camp and my curling iron is dead, heads will roll!"

"We're far enough," Lilly said. "There's a strip mall not far from here that will feed the machine."

McKenna nodded, and pressed a button. A bright electrical display lit her fingertips, and a small milky-white marble, crackling with electricity, appeared in her palm. It grew until it was as big as the whole squad.

"Jackpot, ladies," McKenna said. "This doohickey says there's something gold and valuable on the other side."

"Let's go, girls! We've only got ten minutes," Jeannie said, and she raced directly into the ball and disappeared.

Duncan had explained Gerdie's machine and what it did, but to actually see it was almost more than Matilda's brain could handle. Even with all the tech in the Playground and the millions of tiny robots coursing through her own body, this device still felt like something yanked out of the pages of a comic book.

"Today!" Tiffany barked.

Kylie reached for Matilda's hand. "C'mon, we'll go together."

Matilda and Kylie stepped forward, and then there was a light so bright that Matilda could see it through the hand she raised to protect her eyes. Electricity danced across her skin and an incredible roar flooded her ears. She had once visited Niagara Falls during a mission, and the millions of gallons of water that tumbled over its edge was only half as loud.

And then . . . it was over.

She lowered her hand and glanced around. She and the other cheerleaders were standing inside a dark room with wooden walls and floor. She couldn't see much, but the floor was rocking back and forth.

"We're on a ship," Pammy said.

"Duh," Toni said.

"Can we please not argue?" Shauna said. "We've got nine minutes and counting to grab and go. Unless of course you aren't interested in this room full of treasure chests."

Toni snarled but turned to one of the big wooden chests. She opened the heavy lid and let out a happy shriek.

Matilda stepped forward. Inside the chest, packed to the top, was a collection of gold coins, rubies, sapphires—even a crown. She had never seen anything dazzle so brightly.

"I'm totally posting this!" McKenna said as she reached for her phone. "Hey, there's no service here!"

"So how did we get on a pirate ship?" Matilda asked.

"This is an alternate Earth," McKenna said and gestured to the device on her arm. "This thing built a bridge for us to get here."

Tiffany pushed McKenna aside. "Hello! Eight minutes and counting!"

Matilda watched the squad leap into action like little ferrets stealing seeds. Lilly found a pile of empty canvas sacks and started shoving as much precious material into them as she could. When one was full, she stuffed empty sacks into Matilda's and Kylie's hands and dragged them over to another chest.

"Hey, the first time I did it I was completely freaked out, too. But we don't have a lot of time," Lilly said. "If you don't help, Tiffany might just leave you here."

"The battery is charging at fifty percent, girls," McKenna shouted. "Less talking. More taking!"

Matilda reached into a chest of diamonds, grabbed a handful, and stuffed them into her sack. She felt terrible. She prided herself on her integrity—a trait her parents had instilled in her. How could she ever look them in the eye again? Still, she had to remind herself that this was a mission. She had to do this to save the world—her world.

"Four minutes, people," McKenna said.

"We have to come back here," Shauna said. "There's enough to fund our entire lives. We'd never have to work again."

"We're not here for our retirement. This is for cheerleading only!" Tiffany said. "Besides, the machine doesn't take you back to a world once you've visited it, so you better take what you can."

Just then there was a loud bang. A door slammed opened behind Matilda and she heard a heavy footstep followed by a metallic clink.

Boot-clink. Boot-clink. Boot-clink.

When Matilda turned, she saw a rough-looking man holding the biggest, sharpest sword she had ever seen. His mustache was long and bushy and hung down to his Adam's apple. He was dressed in a black coat embroidered with silver flowers and had a red silken scarf tied around his neck. One of his legs was a stump with nothing more than a crude metal spike for him to balance on. But nothing about his appearance was as shocking as his face. He could have been Agent Brand's twin brother.

"Well, well, what do we have here?" he said.

Matilda shuddered. His voice was identical to her boss's, too.

Another set of feet stomped into the room, this one belonging to a blonde woman. She was tall and lean with braided hair. She had a black patch over her left eye and what looked like the scar of a hangman's noose around her slender neck. Only those two characteristics kept her from being an exact copy of Ms. Holiday. In fact, standing side by side, the pirates looked as if they were Brand and Holiday on their way to a costume party.

"What do we have here, Alex, my lad?" she said, removing a dagger from within her vest.

"Looters, my love," he said. "No-good thieving scoundrels."

"Isn't that what we are, dearest?"

The pirates laughed.

"Indeed. But there has to be some respect for finder's keepers, my darling. This treasure was stolen by us and therefore rightfully belongs to us. It's unbecoming of a scoundrel to steal from other scoundrels."

"I suppose we should alert the captain," the female pirate said.

"Captain?" Matilda asked.

"Someone called?" a voice rang out, and another person entered the room. Matilda's heart almost stopped. The captain was no rogue of the seven seas but eleven-year-old Ruby Peet, dressed in a huge black hat and leather boots, complete with a parrot standing on her shoulder.

"Brand and Holiday! Tell me my eyes don't deceive me! Is it true we have some rats belowdecks? Filthy, thieving vermin. I'm allergic to the hairy little buggers."

"It's true, Captain Peet," Brand said. "Permission to hoist them up by their tails and toss them overboard?"

"No, Brand, this is a pleasure I seize for my own," the pirate Ruby said as she unsheathed a broadsword from her hip. She flashed a rotten smile nearly as deadly as her blade, then charged at Shauna, swinging murderously. The pretty cheerleader screamed and cowered in the corner.

Before Pirate Ruby could slash her throat, Matilda leaped across the tiny room and kicked the sword out of Captain Peet's hand. It clanked to the floor. While Ruby bent to retrieve her weapon, Matilda sucker-punched Brand in the belly. The pirate tumbled over just in time to catch a knee to his front teeth.

"Stay back!" Matilda shouted to the other cheerleaders, though by the looks on their faces they weren't about to attack—or even defend themselves.

"Ye look familiar to me, little one," Pirate Holiday said. "Don't you think so, Captain?"

Peet eyeballed Matilda, rubbing her sword on her shirt. Something flashed in her expression.

"I do," said the captain. "Remember that first mate we had out of Boston? The one with the breathing malady?"

Brand finally regained his breath. "Why, you're right, Captain. She's the spitting image. If I hadn't seen you feed her to the sharks, I'd think it was the same girl."

"Perhaps she's a ghost," the captain said as the two women circled Matilda.

"Take a step closer and I'll show you who's a ghost."

Peet laughed. "Just as chatty as the other one, too. Run her through, Holiday."

Holiday tossed her dagger from hand to hand then charged at Matilda. In such a small space, Matilda couldn't use her inhalers to fly. So instead she turned her stealth inhalers on the woman's face. One squeeze sent the woman flying against the ship's wall, where she crumpled to the floor.

Matilda hoped it looked to the other girls as if she just had a great right hook.

Captain Peet seemed momentarily stunned, but Matilda knew if she was anything like her own Pufferfish, she wouldn't stay that way. Matilda was going to have to fight, and she needed more room.

"Everyone on deck!" Matilda commanded, and the cheerleaders didn't hesitate. They all flew through the door. Kylie and Matilda brought up the rear, tumbling out into the sunshine with the salty air tearing at their eyes and noses.

There they found a dozen more pirates, each filthier than the last. Lilly threw a punch at one Matilda recognized as a member of NERDS' scientific team. Other pirates were alternate versions of teachers from the school, albeit very tough versions. They surrounded the group of girls.

"Whose idea was it to come outside?" McKenna complained.

"Stop complaining and keep an eye on that battery. When it's charged, activate the machine, no matter what is happening!" Matilda said.

"We're at seventy-seven percent right now. I'd say three more minutes. Maybe two."

"Looks like we've flushed us out some worms," a new voice said. Matilda turned and spotted this world's Duncan. He was dressed in striped pants and a huge belt, and he had a red bandanna around his head.

"Awfully pretty worms," Jackson said as he and a pirate version of Flinch joined Duncan. Each of the alternate NERDS wore swords nearly as big as themselves.

"Pretty as gumdrops," Flinch said.

"Keep your eyes in your head," Pirate Peet said as she stomped up on deck. She aimed her sword at the girls. "These ones are fish food. I aim to push them all overboard."

Pammy began to whimper.

Captain Peet cackled. "Any volunteers?"

The pirates laughed.

"What about you?" Peet said, placing her hand on Matilda's shoulder. "Don't worry, girl, the sharks won't come for you right away. They can't smell you unless you're bleeding."

Then with the most murderous face Matilda had ever seen, the pirate ran her sword across Matilda's shoulder. It was just a knick, but it stung enough to make her cry out. A red stain appeared on her shoulder.

"Oops," Captain Peet said, and then she shoved Matilda over the side.

Matilda fell awkwardly and hit the water hard. It was cold and the shock made her gasp. Though it was hard to think, somewhere in her murky mind she remembered that all she had was three minutes until the gate home opened. If she was going back to her world, she needed to time this exactly.

But she'd never see three minutes if she didn't get some air. She fumbled with her utility belt, searching for the right inhalers. She knew the oxygen inhalers were painted blue, but the gray water leeched all color from the plastic. She was struggling to find the right one when something banged into her—something big. She lost her grip on one of the inhalers and watched it tumble into the blackness.

That's when she saw the fins gliding against the bottom of her feet. It was big and gray and fast, and when she saw the flecks of blood floating off her arm she knew exactly what it was: a great white shark.

At the moment, the shark was the least of Matilda's worries. She couldn't breathe. Her lungs were weak to begin with, and her asthma had prevented her from learning to hold her breath for long. Kicking her feet, she rose to the surface. Her head broke through and she gasped for breath. The pirates stood above her on the ship, jeering and laughing.

"How long?" Matilda cried.

"One minute forty seconds," Tiffany shouted back. "And we can't wait for you."

"Nice," Matilda groaned. Her squad mates would not be mounting a rescue.

As she swam toward a rope that dangled from the deck into the water, she saw a shimmer and was dragged down again.

The shark had caught her cheerleading skirt in its jagged teeth, narrowly missing her legs. Their eyes met and she could see the shark's stubborn hunger. There would be no mercy from this fish.

Matilda had fought plenty of full-grown men and one very angry kindergartner, but she didn't have any experience fighting sea life. So she did what came naturally—she punched the shark in the snout. She expected it to cry out—most people did when they were on the receiving end of her uppercuts—but instead it opened its jaws to take a bigger bite. She kicked at it violently, fueled by adrenalin and fear and the desperate desire to not become the shark's breakfast, and managed to knock a few of its many teeth loose. Perhaps somewhere deep in her mind her subconscious took over, because without thinking she reached for her utility belt and snatched whatever inhaler she could. She pushed the plunger, and a blast of concentrated air knocked the shark for a loop. It went spinning out of control with part of her skirt in its jaws.

There was no time to celebrate; her lungs were on fire. Once again, she swam to the shimmering surface and broke through into the air. From there she could see on deck, where the tiny ball of electricity had begun to form in McKenna's hand. If Matilda didn't get back, she would lose her ticket home, and from what Tiffany said, they'd never be able to return to pick her up.

Gripping her inhalers, she was just about to squeeze when

the shark snatched her skirt again. It pulled her down deeper and deeper until she wasn't sure which way was up. This time she knew she only had one chance. As soon as it opened its mouth to take a bite of her, she pushed the plunger on the inhalers and flew.

The shark chased after her, matching her pace. Matilda's heart soared when she saw the streaming sunlight above, and when she broke the surface she gasped in all the air she could. Without stopping, she used the inhalers to sail skyward in a perfect arc up over the railing of the ship and into the milky skin of the glowing portal. A glance back revealed the stunned faces of the pirates. The surprise was enough for the other girls to escape and leap in after her.

When she came out on the other side, she tumbled onto the forest floor and felt the cool night air rushing through her wet, torn clothing. Her lungs were tight and she wheezed in and out violently until she could use her medicinal inhaler. Shivering, she climbed to her feet. Most of the girls looked as if they were in shock. A few were fighting back sobs. And then there was McKenna, who stood over her bag of treasure, texting with lightning speed.

"OMG! I totally missed like a hundred texts. I'll never catch up!"

"Is everyone OK?" Matilda asked.

"Nice job, Maddie," Tiffany said. "You've got moves."

Matilda was red with anger. She wanted to grab the girl and shake the stupidity out of her. These cheerleaders—no, these *children*—were playing with something that they didn't understand. Still, Matilda couldn't blow her cover.

"Yeah. Thanks," she said through clenched teeth. "So, is this something you do a lot?"

Lilly nodded. "We could use someone like you, Matilda."

"No way!" Jeannie shouted. "She shouldn't have confronted those pirates. If she hadn't fought them, we could have just waited for the portal to open and then left."

"If it wasn't for Matilda, we'd all be shark food," Kylie argued.

Tiffany threw her hand up to command their silence. "We need to get back to the cabins. We have practice tomorrow."

Tiffany turned and led the girls back, leaving Matilda behind.

"I'll catch up," she shouted after them.

When she was alone, Matilda considered each of the girls. Which one was Gerdie Baker? McKenna had the device, which made her the top suspect, but Lilly had punched the pirate with a haymaker as good as any she could throw herself. Kylie seemed the bravest during the entire event. Any one of them could be the Mathlete.

When the girls were out of earshot, Matilda tapped her nose to activate the comlink. "I need a medic out here."

A few minutes later the School Bus hovered over the forest. A rope ladder fell and Agent Brand climbed down with a first-aid kit under his arm. He met Matilda by a fallen tree and took a close look at her wound.

"I'm afraid this is going to leave a scar, Wheezer," he said as he removed a needle and thread from the first-aid kit. After stringing the needle, he took a tiny bottle and a syringe from inside the kit. He filled the syringe with liquid and tapped the needle. "I'm not going to lie to you. This might hurt."

Then he jabbed the syringe into her shoulder. She winced and nearly punched him in his handsome face. A second later he was stitching her wound. The injection had killed all the feeling in her arm from her shoulder down.

"I've been to the other side. I had to fight off a bunch of pirates."

"Pirates, huh?"

She nodded. "You were there, you scurvy dog."

"I've seen a lot of odd things, but that's truly strange," he said. "Wonder what I'd do if I came face-to-face with myself. Did you see yourself?"

"Nope," Matilda said. "They'd already pushed the other me overboard."

"This is a nasty cut. I wonder if you are in over your head, Wheezer."

Matilda shook her head. "I'm fine."

"Seven stitches seem to say otherwise," he said as he squeezed some yellow salve onto her wound and dressed it with white bandages. "Not a bad job, if I do say so myself. I don't get to use my field medic skills all that much."

"You were a doctor?"

"A field medic—a military doctor . . . I had a couple years of medical school, but it didn't take. I enlisted, and Uncle Sam puts you in the jobs you are best suited for—so I did it for a few years. I wanted to be a pilot like my brother . . ." He trailed off into his own memories, then came back just as suddenly. "I have no idea what you're going to tell your folks."

"They probably won't notice. They're too busy fighting," Matilda said.

Agent Brand shifted uncomfortably. "Families are hard to keep together. Your mother is OK?"

"She's a statue. It's hard to tell," Matilda said. "My brothers seem fine. It's hard to tell if they're acting out more now than they were before."

"It can help when you have a sibling," Brand said.

There was a long silence between them, as if Mr. Brand

were somewhere else, a place where memories were filled with sharp edges.

Matilda knew she should change the subject.

"Well, I have another concrete suspect," Matilda said.

"Who?"

"McKenna. She's got the bridge device—that's what they're calling it—and she knows how to use it. Give me a couple of hours and I'll go in and arrest her. I'm sure she'll be awake and updating her social media profile, which, by the way, you should probably have Benjamin delete. I'm sure she's just told the whole world she was in another universe."

SUPPLEMENTAL MATERIAL

The following "tweets" are from McKenna Gallagher's Twitter account. There is no real way to calculate how many people may have seen these posts, but they were removed at once.

McKennaOMG McKennaOMG

OMG! I'm totally going 2 another universe today to rob it blind. Hate2BThem!

1 hour ago

McKennaOMG McKennaOMG

Tiff wants 2 bring the new girl . . . ugh.

58 minutes ago

McKennaOMG McKennaOMG

OMG! Almost murdered by py-rats and a shark but the worst part—no cell service 4 10 minutes! I don't know how I survived.

30 minutes ago

McKennaOMG McKennaOMG

Countin' my money. Holla' 4 the dolla' people!

22 minutes ago

McKennaOMG McKennaOMG

Py-rats are scary, yo! Arrrrr.

15 minutes ago

McKennaOMG McKennaOMG
Look at my loot, people. Jealous much?
10 minutes ago

McKennaOMG McKennaOMG
Weird kids in the cabin. One has craz-ee braces.
6 minutes ago

McKennaOMG McKennaOMG
Weird kids are arresting me. So lame!
5 minutes ago

McKennaOMG McKennaOMG
Blindfolded but still txting! Take that nerd kids!
3 minutes ago

McKennaOMG McKennaOMG
I M N A rocket! Craz-eeee!
1 minutes ago

12

38°53' N, 77°05' W

McKenna Gallagher was not happy.
She was locked inside a tiny room with concrete walls and floors. There was no way she could get a signal for her phone—not a single bar! How would anyone know that she had been kidnapped if she couldn't update her Facebook status? Her Twitter followers should know that the room had one exposed lightbulb hanging from a dirty lamp and that it was shining right into her eyes! She needed to let everyone know about the new girl—the Korean-American one with the bad temper—and her gang of nerdy misfits. They had locked her in a basement. This was not LOL! It was SOS!

Maddie sat across from McKenna. "I know you must be confused," she said. She wasn't wearing her cheerleader

uniform anymore. Instead, she had on a black bodysuit that zipped up the front to her neck. If Maddie hadn't kidnapped her, McKenna would probably have told her she looked fierce.

"T 2 the H!" she cried. "You better let me out of here!"

"Pufferfish, what did she say?" Maddie asked.

A girl with superkinky blonde hair stepped forward and opened a laptop. "Just a second. According to my search, she's talking in text messages. 'T 2 the H' means, 'Talk to the hand.'"

"OMGYG2BK!"

"OMGYG2BK?" Maddie asked.

Her friend typed furiously. "Um, just a second. That means 'Oh, my gosh, you've got to be kidding.'" The girl shook her head. "It's like she speaks another language."

"Yeah, it's called annoying," Maddie said, then turned back to McKenna. "Listen, we don't want to waste our time and we don't want to waste yours, so let's just get to the point. It's over. We know who you are."

"LDO!" McKenna said.

"'Like duh, obviously,'" the frizzy blonde translated.

"I was on homecoming court. I'm a cheerleader. I have nine thousand Facebook friends and twelve thousand Myspace friends. I'm topping out at seventeen thousand Twitter followers. Everyone knows me! IMDB!"

The blonde girl started typing. "That means, 'I'm da bomb.'"

"Gerdie, let's—"

"Who? My name's not Gerdie, idiot!"

"We don't need to play this game any longer," Maddie said.

"I hope your parents have great lawyers, 'cause my dad is a crazy great lawyer and he's going to sue you for every penny. H8TBU!"

"'Hate to be you,'" the blonde girl translated.

"Please calm down, Gerdie," the newbie said.

McKenna jumped to her feet and made a dash for the door. "My name's not Gerdie and I will not calm down! Help! Help! Let me out of here!"

Another figure blocked her way. He was cute, with blue eyes and wavy blond hair. But when he smiled—ugh! She remembered him from her abduction—he had a mouth full of metal. Now that he was up close she could see his braces were moving around as if they were alive. They spilled out from between his lips and transformed into huge spindly spider legs and lifted the boy off the ground. McKenna was so shocked she fell backward. Her first instinct was to text Tiffany, but crawling away in a desperate gamble for her life was a close second.

"We're not here to hurt you," Maddie said.

"Help! Help!"

"Gluestick, Flinch?"

A roly-poly boy ran up the side of the wall, then across the ceiling, then down the other side to block her way. Frantically, she scurried to another side of the room, but a jittery Latino kid with a crazy look on his face was blocking that way, too. She turned again only to find him standing there as well. How did he move so fast?

McKenna shook with rage. She stomped her feet, and though later she would feel childish, "I'm telling!" was the first thing that came to mind. Then she reached into her pocket and pulled out her phone.

"I am so posting this!" she snarled.

But she never got a chance. Maddie jumped out of her chair, snatched the phone, and then, much to McKenna's surprise, flew into the air, hovering just out of reach like a bumblebee.

"OMG! You are in big trouble, you freaks!" she shrieked.

"Gerdie—"

"Who is Gerdie?"

"You! You are Gerdie Baker," the girl with the computer said as she held up the bridge device. "And this machine you invented is very dangerous. You're causing all kinds of damage to the national power grid, not to mention all the strange stuff that's getting yanked into our universe."

"UGTBK!"

The girl went back to her laptop. "'You've got to be kidding.'"

"I didn't invent this machine!" McKenna cried. "Do you think I could invent something this complicated? Tiffany gave this to me. She said it didn't go with her eyes. I said it didn't go with mine, either, but she said I had a boxy head and this made it look thinner. I don't even know how that thing works except you push the blue button. There's a gauge on the side that tells you how long you have until the battery is recharged. That's all I know!"

McKenna watched the odd children huddle and whisper. They kept looking over at her suspiciously. She wanted to send frown face texts to them all.

"So Tiffany gave you this?" the chubby one asked. "She invented it?"

"I don't know who invented it, but I highly doubt it was Tiffany. She's as dumb as a box of rocks. I swear her mom sets her clothes out in the morning and has to remind her which are pants and which are tops. Please don't tell her I said that. She can be very mean. SWMBO."

The blonde typed furiously. "'She who must be obeyed.'"

"All I know is it showed up about three weeks ago," McKenna cried in a panic. "It could've come from anyone."

"Well, you've got to get back to the squad," Flinch said to Matilda. "Figure out which of the other girls brought it in."

Matilda shook her head. "This mission is over. We have the device. Let's just toss Texting Tina in some cell for a while until this blows over."

"A cell? Like a jail? I'd never make it. They only let prisoners go online a half hour a week!"

Just then, a man entered the room. He was a hottie, even though he was totally old. McKenna couldn't help but stare at him.

"I'm afraid this mission is far from over, Wheezer. Just because we have this bridge device doesn't mean Gerdie won't build another one. We have to find her so she can help us stop the tears in the universe. They're popping up all over the place now. Agents are telling us they've found a nuclear sub sitting in the middle of that park you girls were in last night. It's not one of ours—the crew was made up of angry beavers."

"I have always suspected the beavers would rise up against us," Jackson said, laughing.

"This is serious business, Braceface. We need to find Gerdie on the double!"

Matilda scowled. "Fine! I'll go back to the stupids and weed out the Mathlete!"

"Who are you calling stupids?!" McKenna snarled.

A pretty woman in glasses stepped into the room. A little blue ball floated in the air behind her. There was so much weirdness around McKenna. Was she losing her mind? She had to stop eating the meatloaf surprise.

"Better leave right away, Wheezer," the woman said. "There has been another tear and something else disappeared."

"What?" Agent Brand asked.

"The Washington Monument."

Brand paused, and then roared, "We have to find a way to stop these tears! Find Gerdie Baker now!"

McKenna almost felt bad for Maddie. She would text her a frownie face if she could. But before she could reach for the phone, a needle was stuck in her arm and she blacked out.

END TRANSMISSION.

THIS NEXT TEST JUDGES HOW YOU
PERCEIVE THE WORLD. DOCTORS CALL THIS
A RORSCHACH TEST. WHAT I WANT YOU TO
DO IS LOOK AT THE PICTURES AND TELL
ME WHICH OF THE FOLLOWING THINGS
YOU SEE IN THEM. HELPFUL HINT: THE
PICTURES ARE NOT TALKING TO YOU. THEY
DON'T TALK. IF YOU HEAR VOICES COMING
FROM THEM, THEN I THINK WE CAN BOTH
AGREE THAT THIS TEST IS OVER.
THEY'RE JUST PICTURES. I PROMISE.

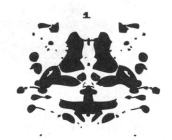

1

a. TWO SEALS GIVING EACH OTHER
   A KISS (3 POINTS)
b. A SPACESHIP FLYING THROUGH
   AN ASTEROID FIELD (3 POINTS)
c. THE BOTTOM OF A BIRDCAGE
   (3 POINTS)

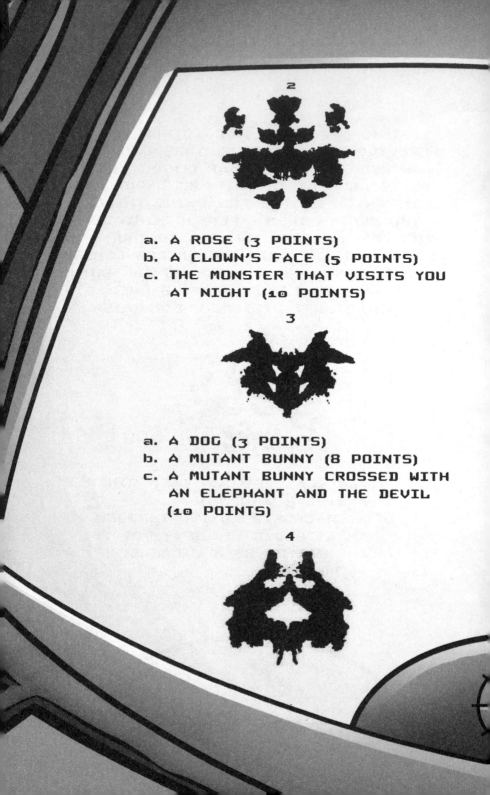

2

a. A ROSE (3 POINTS)
b. A CLOWN'S FACE (5 POINTS)
c. THE MONSTER THAT VISITS YOU
   AT NIGHT (10 POINTS)

3

a. A DOG (3 POINTS)
b. A MUTANT BUNNY (8 POINTS)
c. A MUTANT BUNNY CROSSED WITH
   AN ELEPHANT AND THE DEVIL
   (10 POINTS)

4

a. A WHITE STINGRAY RIDING ON TOP OF A BLACK STINGRAY (5 POINTS)
b. A STEALTH FIGHTER PLANE (3 POINTS)
c. A GREAT SYMBOL FOR MY SUPERVILLAIN COSTUME (9 POINTS)

5

a. A GOOD-LOOKING DUDE (1 POINT)
b. A STAGGERINGLY HANDSOME MAN (1 POINT)
c. MY MORTAL ENEMY (10 POINTS)

TOTAL THEM UP, BUSTER.

_____

WOW. SCARY.

ACCESS GRANTED

BEGIN TRANSMISSION:

13

38°85' N, 77°08' W

McKenna was given a memory drug that erased the last twenty-four hours of her life, which saved Matilda's cover story and allowed her to continue her search for Gerdie Baker. Getting both of the girls back into the camp, however, was no easy task. McKenna slobbered like a bulldog and her legs were jelly, but Matilda somehow managed to pull her along. She dumped the dozing cheerleader onto her bunk and shoved her cell phone into her hand the way one might give a toddler a security blanket. Then Matilda fell into bed herself and slept as deeply as she ever had.

She woke from a dream in which her family—her mother, father, and brothers—were all living happily under the same roof. Ben and Molly waltzed around the living room, twirling

like tops, smiling and gazing into each other's eyes. Waking up to the real world felt like a body slam, and Matilda sat staring out the window next to her bunk and trying not to cry. She wondered if she could use Gerdie's bridge device to find the world of her dreams. A simple push of a button could take her to a place where her mom and dad still loved each other.

When she felt calmer, she decided to take advantage of the fact that everyone else was still asleep. She climbed out of the bunk and moved from cabin to cabin, quietly searching through Lilly's, Kylie's, and Pammy's belongings. She opened their drawers and duffel bags, rifled through their personal things, even peeked under their beds. Unfortunately, she didn't find anything useful, except that Pammy might be a candy hoarder.

Frustrated, Matilda put everything back in place and returned to her bunk. She flipped open her notebook and took stock of her notes. Her suspects were mysteries to her. Kylie was kind and funny and in a crisis she kept a cool head. She could certainly have learned that from spy training. Tiffany was very athletic, something that would have come in handy as a secret agent. On the other hand, there were Pammy and Lilly, who spent most of their hours in front of the mirror, complimenting themselves. They followed Tiffany around like puppy dogs, and both could be exceptionally mean, but these were all just surface observations. What did she really know about them? Nothing! They were almost strangers to her. Kylie was sweet—she could even possibly be a real friend to Matilda—but getting to know the others made Matilda cringe. With her friends at home she had complete confidence, and she wasn't bashful about speaking to anyone. But here, at this camp, with her makeup and cheerleading skirt, she felt awkward. Odd how suddenly becoming what most people thought of as beautiful and popular made her feel like a nerd. If only she could swap out the lip gloss for her combat boots!

She managed to catch a few more minutes of sleep before she felt someone standing over her. Pammy was fully dressed in her cheerleading outfit with her arms crossed and a scowl on her face.

"Cheerleaders can't be lazy," she snapped.

"Um, tired! Attacked by pirates—almost eaten by a shark!"

Pammy rolled her eyes. "Boo-hoo! Let me play a sad violin for you! Get dressed."

Matilda swallowed her impulse to deliver a roundhouse kick to the snotty girl and instead called out to her. "Listen, I know we don't know each other well, but maybe we could be friends."

"Friends? You've been watching too much *Sesame Street*," Pammy said.

"I don't know the first thing about you," Matilda said. She tried to remember Gerdie's file. What had it said about her sisters? Were they triplets? Yes! "Like, do you have any brothers or sisters?"

Pammy turned and looked at Matilda for a long time, then sighed in surrender. "No, I'm an only child. My parents wisely decided to spend all their time and money to make me the amazing person that I am today. Now, if you've got enough info for your biography, you better get outside and be ready to cheer in five minutes!"

As Pammy stomped out of the cabin, Matilda jotted in her notebook that she was an only child. She tucked the notebook under her pillow, then leaped out of bed. A moment later she was dressed and rushing outside. She hoped that Tiffany would notice her eagerness and not abuse her as much as usual; her mostly sleepless night was starting to catch up to her. She also hoped she'd have a chance to talk to her other suspects, especially Lilly and Kylie. Unfortunately, she was the last one to arrive for practice. Lilly was propping up McKenna, as the effects of the memory wipe were clearly still causing balance problems, and poor Kylie was forced to follow Tiffany around with a hot cup of cocoa in case their leader needed a sip.

"I thought Pammy told you to get ready!" Tiffany snapped at Matilda.

"What? I am ready!"

Tiffany laughed. "Your hair is ugh and where's your makeup? When we practice, we have to look like we're going on stage. You may think you're a natural beauty, but I promise you that you're not. Oh, and take Kylie. She could use some work, too."

Matilda enjoyed a beautiful little daydream about body slamming Tiffany into the muddy practice field, but she also realized that their leader was doing her a favor. Now she would get some alone time with one of her suspects.

Matilda and Kylie stood in front of the bathroom mirror. They debated blush and eyeliner while Matilda pretended to know the difference between them.

"So you're makeup challenged, too?" Kylie said.

Matilda nodded. "I wasn't exactly a girlie-girl before cheerleading entered my life."

Kylie smiled. "Nice to know someone else was going through an awkward phase."

"Awkward, huh?"

"The worst. Sometimes I wondered if I was even human—but hey, look at me now. I'm hot!" She licked her finger, set it on her arm, and then made a sizzling sound.

"I'm so hot I have a fever!" Matilda said. She couldn't help but like Kylie. Unlike the other girls, who seemed proud of how shallow and superficial they could be, Kylie had a sense of self that couldn't be touched by petty insults. She didn't seem to care what the others thought of her.

"So, where are you from, Kylie?"

"Oh, everywhere. My mom moves us around a lot. You?"

"Well, I was born in San Francisco but moved east when I was a baby. My parents wanted me to get a good education. I'm a bit of a math prodigy. Do you like math?"

Kylie smiled. "I can barely add two plus two," she said. "And I wouldn't walk around bragging about being smart in front of the rest of the squad. There's nothing that makes dumb people angrier than having a smart person reminding them that they're morons."

"HEY!" Tiffany's voice bellowed from outside. "Let's go! The portal is opening right now!"

How is that possible? Matilda thought. She and the NERDS had confiscated it.

They raced into the forest and saw Toni and Jeannie vanishing into the huge white ball. This time, Shauna was wearing a bridge device, brand-new and just as pink and sparkly as the last.

Tiffany and McKenna were in the midst of a heated argument as more girls disappeared into the portal.

"I'm sorry!" McKenna cried, though somewhat sleepily.

"How do you lose a machine that opens a door to other Earths?" Tiffany shouted. "Do you think these things grow on trees?"

"Where did you get that one?" Matilda asked.

"Don't you worry about where I got it, newbie!" Tiffany said. "Just get through the portal!"

Matilda and Kylie did as they were told. In a flash the camp was gone and they were tumbling into a humid rain forest. Ancient trees soared overhead, while a gurgling stream slipped over a stone riverbed. Insects as big as Matilda's fist buzzed around the girls' heads.

"Um, I think there's supposed to be treasure," Jeannie complained. "Whose idea was it to let Shauna use the glove?"

"Harsh! The scanner said there's a temple in this forest with a huge stockpile of gold," Shauna said defensively.

"Pair up and spread out," Tiffany said. "The temple has to be close by."

"I'll go with Lilly," Matilda said. She could tell Kylie was a little hurt, but when major landmarks were vanishing from Washington, D.C., you had to have priorities.

Lilly seemed just as put out, but Matilda ignored it. She looped her arm through the girl's and marched her into the brush.

"I thought we could use the time to get to know each other," Matilda said.

"Whatever," Lilly said.

"So, Lilly, tell me about yourself," Matilda said.

"What do you care? Are you spying on me?"

"Of—of course not," Matilda stammered.

"Everyone on this squad is the same—two-faced. I hate how we all gang up on each other, and I'm sure anything I tell you will just get used against me when Queen Tiffany decides to dole out her favors."

"I promise I'm not out to get you," Matilda said. "Just making conversation."

"You're actually interested?"

Matilda nodded. "Sure."

"You first then. Tell me something about yourself that you

don't want anyone to know. You spill and I'll spill," Lilly said, swatting at a rather large jungle beetle.

"I have six brothers."

"Wow, it must have been very painful to tell me that," Lilly said.

"OK. OK!" Matilda said. She didn't want to tell this stranger her deep, dark secrets, but if it would get her to open up . . . "My parents are going to get a divorce and I cry at night sometimes hoping they will get back together."

"They won't," Lilly said flatly. "My parents are divorced, too. They even tried to get back together. It's just not going to happen."

"Is that why you're angry?"

Lilly took a step back. "You think I'm angry?"

Matilda nodded.

"Yeah, I guess I am," Lilly said.

Matilda knew from Gerdie's file that her parents were divorced. Could Lilly be the Mathlete? Did she have sisters? Did she ever live in Arlington?

Just then, something brown and hairy leaped down from the trees above their heads. It was a chimpanzee, but not like any she had seen in a zoo. This one was wearing a strange harness that covered his chest, legs, and arms. He was also carrying a bushel of bananas under one of his stringy arms. He eyed the cheerleaders carefully, and then, much to Matilda's shock, he tapped his nose and said, "Flinch here. I have found two of the invaders."

He quickly peeled a handful of bananas and shoved them into his mouth. As he chewed, his harness began to glow. He pounded on his chest and shouted, "I am mighty!"

Matilda peered closely at the creature. This chimpanzee was Flinch—a very hairy version, but Flinch nonetheless. There was Flinch's harness, and the sugar, and the chimp was even shouting his catchphrase. And he wasn't alone. Soon, a cute yellow monkey no bigger than a house cat swung through the trees by its tail. By the way it was scratching its arms and legs, Matilda guessed it was this world's Ruby Peet. An orangutan leaped from tree to tree as if its feet and hands were covered in glue—obviously Duncan. Rushing up behind them was a baboon Jackson Jones, with a bright red nose, blue face, and enormous robotic appendages coming from its mouth. But the most startling was the razorback gorilla that flew overhead with the help of two tiny inhalers.

The animals stepped into their fighting stances and surrounded the girls.

"Stay where you are," the little yellow monkey commanded. "We're waiting for your machine to recharge and then you and the rest of you moronic girls are going back to where you belong."

Lilly cringed. "Talking monkeys!"

The gorilla pounded her chest and bared her fangs. "Some of us are apes!" she said, clearly insulted.

"Run!" Lilly cried, hurling herself into the overgrown jungle.

"Wait!" Matilda shouted, but Lilly was already gone. Matilda chased after her, swatting at branches and leaves. Roots sprang up on the path and snakes slithered out of her way. It seemed as if the whole jungle had risen up to torment her, but she eventually caught up with Lilly just as they plowed into Tiffany and McKenna.

"What is wrong with you nutcases?" Tiffany said.

"Monkeys are attacking!" Lilly cried.

"She's gone crazy," McKenna said. "I have to post about her breakdown!"

Just then the razorback flew overhead, propelled by two rocket-fueled inhalers. The rest of the furry team followed, causing Tiffany and McKenna to join in Lilly's panic. The three of them ran off, once again abandoning Matilda.

Matilda stood up, brushed herself off, and shouted up into the trees. "You want to talk, I'm right here, but make it quick. We've got less than ten minutes before the portal opens and we have to leave!"

The gorilla slammed down hard in front of her, and the other creatures swung into view. The tiny yellow one leaped onto the gorilla's shoulder and cleared her throat.

"Humans that talk," the monkey said.

"Fascinating," the baboon said.

"I've never been this close to a human," the chimpanzee Flinch said. "She's quite stinky."

The orangutan stepped forward and eyed her closely. "The talking must be some trick she picked up. She's mimicking us. The one at the zoo does tricks, too."

The baboon Duncan fell from a tree and landed on his feet. "I don't think it's a trick. She appears to be intelligent."

"You do realize I'm standing right here and can hear every word you say," Matilda grumbled.

"I'd hardly call her intelligent," a voice said from above, and then another creature landed at her feet. This one looked almost catlike, with a long striped tail. Matilda knew they were called lemurs—at least on her Earth. It peered into her face curiously.

"Not as smart as you, Mathlete, but still bright for her species," the baboon said.

"Wait! You're the Mathlete?" Matilda said to the lemur. "I mean, you're this world's Mathlete? I'm not from here."

"Clearly," the monkey Ruby said.

"But I'm one of you, I mean, I'm part of NERDS, but on my Earth. Wow, this is really hard to explain. My name is Matilda Choi. They call me Wheezer."

"No way!" The razorback gorilla sneered and then circled her, eyeing her up and down. "There is no way I would be a cheerleader! Not on any planet."

It was then that Matilda noticed the gorilla had a unibrow.

The lemur hopped up onto a branch. "We understand you are from somewhere else. Do you understand your visit here is destroying the multiverse?"

"You're experiencing it here, too?"

"We've had some tearing in the fabric of reality. Things have been slipping into our world. If it hadn't been for MISFIT, we would have no idea what was happening. I presume you are working with them?"

"MISFIT?"

"The Multiverse and Interdimensional Special Forces Intelligence Team," the orangutan said. "They're a version of NERDS from Earth 1. They fight crimes across the multiverse."

Matilda was bewildered. "Well, we could use their help. We're trying to stop this on our own. Did they tell you that the human version of Mathlete is responsible for all this chaos?"

"Harrumph," the lemur said.

"Garrrrughhggaaa," the chimpanzee Flinch said, overcome by the sugar in the bananas. He turned the knob on his harness. "What are you doing to stop her?"

"I have to find her first. We don't know what she looks like," Matilda said, then turned to the lemur. "Listen, I know this is a bit of a long shot, but if you can tell me anything about yourself that might help me identify my Gerdie, it could help. You are obviously very different, but I'm desperate!"

The lemur shook her head.

Suddenly, there was a loud hum. Matilda knew exactly what it was. The bridge device had activated.

"You need to get to the portal," the orangutan said, echoing her thoughts.

"Fix this problem, human," the lemur said. "Your world is not the only one at stake."

Before Matilda left, she turned once more to her primate self. The gorilla eyed her right back. Then Matilda ran into the forest toward the device's noise. She found the rest of the squad climbing down the stairs of what looked like an ancient Mayan pyramid. The five-story hand-crafted stone structure rose high above the jungle floor, and she spotted a small ceremonial room at its top. By the looks of the heavy sacks the girls were carrying down its steps, that's where the treasure was stored.

"Glad to see the monkeys didn't eat you," Lilly said.

Matilda nodded. "Me, too."

"You can forget about running up there and getting any of the gold. The portal is open. You blew it running around like a freak in the jungle," Tiffany said, walking past her toward the glowing silver ball.

"H82BU," McKenna said.

Matilda pretended to be disappointed. In the last twenty-four hours she had nearly been killed by pirates, had nearly been eaten by a great white shark, and had come face-to-face with a gorilla version of herself. The crazy level had been turned up to ten! But all of these run-ins would be much preferable to what she had to do next. If she wanted to find Gerdie, she was going to have to do something drastic, and just the thought of it made her cringe.

14

Screwball's feet were bound together and his arms were wrapped in a straitjacket. The heavy chain tied around his chest was equipped with fifteen industrial-strength padlocks that would require a blowtorch to cut. He had a mask over his face to prevent him from biting, and he was strapped to a wheelchair. The asylum staff had taken these precautions since he was being visited by someone whose name had appeared on a list he'd made entitled "10 People I Want to Watch Die." The list read:

1. Duncan Dewey
2. Jackson Jones
3. Julio Escala
4. Ruby Peet

5. Agent Alexander Brand

6. The smug man on the Food Network who bakes extreme cakes

7. The dog whisperer

8. Santa Claus, for a lifetime of disappointments

9. Matilda Choi

10. To be decided . . . but probably someone I really hate

With Matilda sitting directly across from him, he realized it had been a stupid list to make, especially with his new plan in full swing. Now he had to turn on the charm, which is not easy when you are tied up like a wild animal.

"Old friend! So nice of you to come visit me in the loony bin," he said. His guard unfastened the padlocks chaining Screwball's hands together and ran the chains down to the floor and through two steel pins mounted there. Then he snapped the locks shut. "I hope you'll excuse my outfit. It appears the hospital staff thinks I'm dangerous." He leaned forward as far as the chains would allow. "I know. Silly, huh?"

He laughed in hopes that she would join him, but she sat there stone-faced.

"I'm here because . . . I need your help," Matilda said. She winced as she said the words.

Screwball couldn't help himself. He let loose his all-new, all-sinister laugh. It started out slow but soon rose to a headache-inducing whine. He laughed so hard his stomach hurt. If he

hadn't been chained to the chair, he might have rolled up in a
ball and guffawed all day. From the sour look on Matilda's face

and her clenched fists, he could see he had finally perfected it. So much for playing the nice guy.

Matilda cleared her throat. "We want to know everything you know about—"

"Gertrude Baker?" Screwball said.

Her face fell, and he broke into another round of wicked giggles. "Or, as we used to call her, Mathlete. Brilliant girl. Her skills with numbers were even superior to mine after she got her upgrades. Seems the nanobytes allowed her to process information much faster than a normal human brain—I was quite envious. She and I were new recruits together, you know, but she wasn't around long. Her family moved to Ohio."

"Then you know what she's built?" Matilda asked.

Heathcliff chuckled. "I should. I helped her."

He watched her face grow red with rage. "That machine is threatening the world!"

"Oh, is it becoming a nuisance?" Screwball said in a baby voice. "I'm soooo sowwy, but I'm afwaid it's going to get much, much worse."

"Play games with me and I will fly you up ten thousand feet and let go!"

Screwball winced. He wasn't sure if it was a threat or a promise. Matilda had always been unpredictable. "There's no need to resort to violence. Ask yourself, why would I help someone build a machine that allows you to visit the multiverse?

Is it just to create problems? Cause a few power outages?"

"You're rambling, Heathcliff. I'm powering up my inhalers right now!"

Without warning, he felt his blood boil. He lunged forward, chains rattling. "My name is not Heathcliff!"

"Sorry, Choppers," Matilda said.

"Wrong!"

"Right, so what was it? Oh yeah—Simon."

He snarled. "I've cast off that name as well for a more appropriate moniker. You may call me Screwball! Isn't that hilarious? You see! I'm in a mental hospital for the criminally insane. I'm completely cuckoo! You get it, right? Right?"

"I don't care if you call yourself John Jacob Jingleheimer Schmidt!" Matilda said. "Tell me what you've done!"

Screwball took a deep breath and sat back down. "Wheezer, relax. If I have learned anything from my stay in here it's that you need to just chill out."

"Every second we sit in here the bridge device is making things worse outside," she said.

"But you've got it all wrong, agent. Gerdie's machine doesn't build a bridge to other worlds. It pushes the worlds apart. That's what's causing all the troubles."

"Can everyone in the world just for one moment pretend that I am not a supergenius," Matilda said, slamming her fist on the table.

"Touchy, touchy. By now I'm sure you've heard that there are billions, maybe even trillions, of Earths that exist in their own dimensions. What you probably don't know is that all these Earths exist in the exact same place in those dimensions. It's called the universal constant—Earth's location is the only place that is the same in every dimension. When Gerdie turns on her machine, it shoves the Earths around, knocking them out of the constant, and when that happens it stretches the multiverse and sometimes even tears it, creating a hole from our world to another. That's what's causing all the crazy phenomena, Wheezer. Her machine is making Swiss cheese out of our dimension."

"So if we find the machine and never turn it on again, everything will go back to normal?" Matilda asked.

"Nope," Screwball said, he smiled behind his mask. "The first time Gerdie turned on her machine, she pushed our world hopelessly out of alignment. It's floating outside the constant. The more times she uses it, the worse it gets, but even if you never turned it on again, the holes would still be there. In fact, they'll probably just get bigger."

Matilda was silent. He could see her trying to understand what he had said.

"Which will destroy the world," he added helpfully.

"Yeah, I kind of figured that out," Matilda said. "How do we stop this?"

Screwball rubbed his hands together eagerly. His scheme was

working exactly as planned. "You can't. Only I can. You have to release me from this hospital."

"Yeah, right!" Matilda cried. "I'm not letting your crazy behind out of here. You'll just try to take over the world again."

"Matilda! I am shocked. Can't you see I'm a changed person?"

Matilda eyed him disapprovingly.

Screwball laughed. "OK, fine. Busted! But I'm your only hope. I can build a machine that will put our universe back where it belongs. It's your choice."

Matilda tapped her nose to activate her comlink. "Have you been listening?"

Screwball watched her, listening to what he guessed was a lively argument.

"He can't be trusted!" she said, then frowned. She tapped her nose once more to turn off the communication device.

"We have a deal," she said. "You'll be under twenty-four-hour surveillance and in the custody of the team. You will get to work on this new machine, but know this—if you try to pull any shenanigans, I will drop you in a volcano."

"I consider myself warned," he said, though he couldn't help but grin. His plan was working—but then again, he was a genius. Of course it was working! "Oh, and Matilda, I do have a few demands. Nothing a secret society of spies should have a problem acquiring . . ."

EVIDENCE: The following is a letter detailing the demands of former agent Heathcliff Hodges, also known as Choppers, also known as Simon, also known as Screwball, in exchange for his saving the multiverse.

Attention, Lesser Beings,

It has come to my attention that you require my help. Let me start by saying . . . Ha!

I knew this day would come. Double ha!

But there will be enough time to gloat later (trust me, it will occur). There is work to be done! To get started, I have compiled this list of demands. I've taken the liberty of putting them into two categories: Deal Breakers and Wish List. As you can imagine, Deal Breakers are must-haves; the others I would enjoy, and obtaining them would go a long way toward your continued survival when I inevitably take over this planet.

Deal Breakers

1. I want to be released from this hospital.
2. I want my goon to accompany me. Please call his service and inform him that his presence is required.
3. I want all my enemies to be destroyed.

Wish List

1. I tire of kittens. Find a place to put them and never let me see one again!
2. I want a lifetime supply of the delicious candy treat

called Circus Peanuts. All of the people who think they are gross should be pushed into the ocean so I never have to see someone give me that look of revulsion when I sit and idly eat an entire sack of them.

3. I want my driver's license, and yes, I know I am only eleven, but I still want it.
4. I want to be able to carry a bazooka with me wherever I go.
5. I want someone to carry the bazooka for me when it gets heavy.
6. It would be totally awesome of you to give me back my upgrades so I can take over the world ;) Just kidding!
7. I want a major city in this country to change its name to Screwball City and this major city cannot be in Pennsylvania, Rhode Island, or Alaska.
8. When I went rogue, my parents' memory of me was erased. I want them to remember who I am.

Your lord and (inevitable) master,
Screwball

Official Note: After careful review, most of Screwball's requests were denied. We recommend close supervision of Mr. Hodges—anyone who likes those icky Circus Peanut candies cannot be right in the head.

An hour later Screwball was taken out of the hospital. Unfortunately, he had missed lunch—and it was taco day.

"If I am going to save the world, the very least you can do is feed me," Screwball said as he was led in chains through the halls of Nathan Hale Elementary. Of course he knew he was a prisoner and responsible for the calamity that threatened to tear apart the universe, but would it have killed them to go through a drive-through or something?

"The cafeteria's closed, bub," the lunch lady said. The big brawny brute was escorting him, along with Pufferfish, Braceface, Flinch, Wheezer, Gluestick, and his goon.

"I will have tacos!" he pouted. "Pizza! A hot dog! I must feed my body and mind!"

"Kid, if you don't calm down, I'm going to feed you this chain," the lunch lady growled.

At once, the goon stepped forward and the two men shot each other deadly stares.

"You feeling froggy, pal?" the lunch lady said. "Why don't you take a leap?"

The goon flashed his hooked hand.

"Am I supposed to be afraid? What are you going to do, open a can of SpaghettiOs on me?" the lunch lady asked.

"Calm down, my friend," Screwball said to the goon.

"Listen to Nutball," the lunch lady said.

"It's Screwball!"

"Does it matter?" the lunch lady argued. "Tell your paid monkey not to be fooled by the dress. I got a right hook that feels like a hammer."

"Let's just get these two into the Playground, please," Pufferfish said. "My feet are swelling up. Something dangerous is about to happen."

"What do you think is causing it?" Braceface said.

"I think it's radiation!" Pufferfish said. "I felt it when we met those talking dogs, and it's all over Wheezer."

"So, I'm radioactive?" Wheezer said. "Great! Couldn't that be what you're reacting to?"

Pufferfish shook her head. "Nope. This is bigger."

"Graggghhh?" Flinch said, then turned the knob on his harness to calm himself. "Do you think it's one of those tears?"

"Then we must get away," Screwball said. He knew as well as anyone that dangerous things could step through those tears, and the NERDS were stupid enough to want to stay and fight whatever it was.

"What's the matter, Hodges?" Jackson said. "Are you afraid you might have to face the consequences of your invention?"

Suddenly, a bright light appeared in the air in front of them in the hallway. An ear-shattering boom sent Screwball falling backward. He had only imagined the tears and had not seen one in person. It was both frightening and exciting at the same time. He could feel its raw power all around him.

"I hope whatever comes out of that hole eats you!" Matilda shouted.

Just then a battalion of figures dressed in strange silver suits raced out of the hole. At first glance they appeared human, but as the light from the tear dimmed, Screwball could see they were shaped more like gigantic grasshoppers. Their faces were flat and green with black, bulbous eyes. Two spindly antennae poked out of their foreheads, and their mouths were nothing but pinchers. Each held a strange weapon attached to tubes that led to tanks strapped on their shoulders.

"Looks like we've got an infestation of humans, people. Prepare for spraying," one of the bugs said.

"Try to keep them in the hallway. If they get loose, they can go back to their lair and lay eggs. We all know what a hassle it is to clean them out," another one said.

"Ugh, the contract said it was just some vermin. Not humans! We should get them on the phone and tell them it's going to cost more. I don't want anyone complaining about the bill when it comes," a third bug said.

"I've heard these things are practically indestructible. They say they could survive a nuclear bomb. Filthy little things could crawl under a refrigerator and live until the end of time. Spray them!"

The bugs fired their weapons, spraying every corner of the hallway with a thick green liquid. Screwball couldn't help but scream, and later he would feel embarrassed, but these were bugs—he hated bugs. Talking ones were even freakier. Luckily, the usually dimwitted Jackson sprang into action using his braces to build a shield that protected everyone from the toxic chemical.

Suddenly, the bugs were shouting at one another to stop the spraying.

"What kind of pest has its own force field, boss?" one of them asked.

"It must be a new strain! Keep spraying!"

The bugs continued their extermination with the same result.

"You have to stop this!" Screwball shouted at Pufferfish.

"Me? This is your fault!"

"Wait, did one of them talk? Guys, we're not getting paid enough for this nonsense. You get that fat beetle on the phone and tell him we don't do this kind of work. Humans that talk and have force fields need the military—not exterminators."

"Nonsense!" another said. "It doesn't matter what they can do; we were paid to clear them out. Get the flamethrower ready."

"Flamethrower!" Screwball cried as he scurried behind his goon. "My friend, this is a perfect time for us to prove our trustworthiness. We need to sacrifice ourselves to save the others."

"That's genius, boss," the goon said. "What do ya suggest?"

"Leap out and attack them," Screwball said.

"Um, they're shooting poison at us."

"It will appear very brave," he said. "Naturally, I will command you to do it, which will make them believe I have good intentions."

"Where is the 'we' in this sacrifice?" the goon asked.

"Someone has to stay back to make sure the other's sacrifice properly celebrated," Screwball explained. "These fools are not smart enough to understand how selfless we're being, and I will be there to remind them."

"Why can't I do the reminding and youse do the attacking?" the goon grumbled.

"I would be happy to go! But tragically, I'm locked in chains, if you haven't noticed. Can you even imagine the envy I have that you will be saving the day? Now, enough rubbing my nose in it. Go save us—but wait for my heroic command!"

The goon sighed.

"Minion! Stop these monsters and save us all!" Screwball shouted, then watched as the goon jumped into the fray. He punched one of the insects, then kicked another in its armored belly. He used his hook to slash the hoses that led to the poison tanks and had nearly wiped them all out when he turned and found a weapon pointed right in his face.

"I hate you creepy-crawly things!" the bug shouted and sprayed him in the face.

The goon screamed and clawed at his eyes. "I can't see!"

Screwball watched as his former teammates leaped to the goon's defense. Flinch snatched the giant bug and tossed him into the gaping, bright energy hole. Braceface used his shield to push others back, and Pufferfish leaped up, planting her foot into another's face.

The rest of the bugs fled, running headfirst into the light, vanishing into nothing as the hole shrank and disappeared.

"We've got to get this one to the infirmary," the lunch lady said, as he hefted the goon over his shoulder.

Screwball saw his employee's face was red and swollen, covered in horrible blisters. He was a mess! What luck! He couldn't have planned it better himself.

"Did you see what I did, old friends?" Screwball asked. "Did you see the sacrifice I made? I commanded my only companion to save us all. I hope that you will see how courageous that was of me. Clearly, I'm trustworthy."

Everyone stared at him in disbelief.

Could they really not see his sacrifice? "I was quite heroic commanding my goon to save us—selfless, you could say."

They continued to stare.

"Really! I'm without a goon now. Do you know what it feels like for an evil genius to be without a goon? It's like being naked!"

They continued down the now-empty hall and stopped in front of a row of lockers. They opened the doors, stepped inside, and were whisked downward several stories until they reached the Playground. A team of medics carried the goon away. Benjamin zipped over and hovered around Screwball like an angry wasp.

"So, you're back," the orb chirped. "Just so you know, I have my fiber-optic eye on you. You can't be trusted. In fact, I can sense your heartbeat is elevated, proving that you are lying."

"I didn't say anything!" Screwball said.

"You don't have to!" Benjamin replied.

Agent Brand and Ms. Holiday were waiting there as well. The rugged director stepped forward to address the staff of scientists standing in a group. "Attention, everyone! As you can see, Heathcliff has returned to help us with our current dilemma. You are to give him your complete cooperation, but let's make something perfectly clear. Mr. Hodges is not to be trusted. If he is meddling in things he should not be, then alert security and me at once."

"What a lovely introduction," Screwball grumbled. "I feel so welcome."

Brand turned to him. "All right, kid, you've got the finest scientific minds at your disposal. You have space-age technology and materials. It's time to get to work."

"What I want to build is complicated, and most of these so called 'brilliant minds' are nothing more than monkeys in lab coats. I don't have the time or inclination to explain to them the science behind my plans. It's best to put me in the upgrade chair, give me back my teeth, and then I can control them all. Hypnotizing them to do the work is really the most efficient approach."

"You're not getting anywhere near the upgrade room," Matilda said.

Heathcliff was indignant. "You came to me for help!"

"I want guards on the upgrade room twenty-four hours a day," Brand shouted. "No one goes in or out—not even team members."

"I see," Screwball said as he scowled. His anger got the best of him, and before he knew it he was turning red and shouting vicious threats at everyone. Soon he found himself strapped to a heavy chair.

The blue orb zoomed over to him and hovered in front of his face. "Now that you're comfortable, we should get started."

Screwball fumed. "To counteract Gerdie Baker's machine, I am proposing we build something of our own. I call it 'the atomic harpoon.' In its simplest form we're going to use a rope of tightly packed subatomic material which we will fire at our Earth from another dimension. We will build a second harpoon, as well, that we'll activate here. The two harpoons will reel us back into the universal constant. Once we're back in place the crisis will be over."

"Fascinating," Duncan said.

"That's an incredible understatement, Duncan. It's nothing short of enlightened. This plan cements my standing as the most important mind in this universe . . . or any other!" Screwball bragged.

Duncan rolled his eyes. "How long will it take for you to build it?"

"Oh, it would take me thousands of years to build it," Screwball said.

"All right!" Brand shouted. "You're going back to the hospital!"

Screwball was surprised by the spy's anger. "This machine is theoretical and the math necessary for it to work is beyond anything anyone can do. No one is more frustrated than me. Imagine being a genius and fully aware of your limitations! It's bumming me out!"

"THEN WHY ARE YOU HERE?" Brand cried.

"Because it's not beyond the brainpower of Gerdie Baker, or at least not beyond that of the Mathlete. Bring in Gerdie and give her back her upgrades. Her supercharged brain will help me assemble my invention."

"Absolutely not!" Pufferfish said.

"Gerdie's upgrades are essential!" Heathcliff said. "I can't build it without her."

"We can't find her!" Wheezer cried, then used her inhaler. "She's changed her appearance. She doesn't look anything like she did."

"The answer is rather obvious. It's math," Screwball said.

"Math?"

"She loves math," he said. "No! Love is the wrong word. She's obsessed with math. Gerdie can't help herself. If there's a problem, she has to solve it—and the more complicated the better. She'll give herself away with the right equation."

"If we bring you Gerdie, is it going to take thousands of years?" Brand asked.

Screwball shook his head. "Together we can build it in no time at all. Gluestick and Pufferfish can activate one of the machines here. Gerdie and I will go to the other Earth to set it up there."

Screwball watched Brand stew in his anger. "Wheezer, time is running out. We need Gerdie Baker and we need her right now!"

Matilda sighed and turned to Duncan. "I need the hardest math equation you can find."

15

 38°85' N, 77°08' W

Matilda slipped back into camp while the girls were eating breakfast. They had hardly noticed she was gone.

"No eggs?" she grumbled as she sat next to the others at one of the picnic tables outside. Her tray was covered in the four *b*'s: broccoli, brown rice, bean curd, and blech!

"Jeannie's vegan," Kylie explained as she sipped on her ginger bean-curd soup. "And Toni thinks breakfast food gives her pimples."

Matilda sniffed her rice and stuck out her tongue. She picked at it until only Kylie was left at the table.

"You don't enjoy this, do you?" Kylie said.

"I'm sort of a pancakes, waffles, sausage, eggs, and more sausage kind of girl," Matilda replied.

"Not the food, silly. Cheerleading," Kylie said.

Matilda froze. Ms. Holiday had warned her about staying positive around the other girls. Cheerleaders were usually happy people. Had her early disdain for her mission painted her as a grouch?

"I get it," Kylie said. "I wouldn't want to be here if my parents were splitting up, either."

"What?"

"Lilly told me you're upset about it. Mine broke up, too. You're probably doing this whole cheerleading thing to get attention."

Matilda nodded. She didn't know where this conversation was going, and she didn't necessarily agree with Kylie, but as long as one of her suspects was talking she would let her.

"My mom and dad got so caught up in fighting they sometimes forgot how confused I was. The only way to get their attention was to throw myself into cheering. My mom did it when she was my age. My dad said he met her at a game. Once I showed a little interest in it, they showed a lot more interest in me. Still, I feel like a fraud sometimes. The skirts and the hair aren't really me. I'm kind of a tomboy."

"I've been accused of the same thing," Matilda admitted.

"I turned myself into someone my mom and dad could get excited about—and the fighting stopped . . . a little. I know lots of kids who did the same thing. They got into sports, or art, or whatever. I know this kid back home who started dressing like a misfit just so his parents would worry about him. He had a pair of combat boots he never took off—he even wore them to bed." Kylie smiled sadly. "We all do what we have to, I guess."

Matilda couldn't speak. Suddenly, she didn't feel much like a secret agent. She was supposed to be collecting information on Kylie and the others, but her friend seemed to be the one with all the understanding. Matilda's strange clothes, the wrestling, the Ultimate Fighting—it had all been an effort to get Molly and Ben to stop arguing.

When her nanobytes helped her asthma, there was nothing to keep her mom and dad busy. The crazy clothes and hair had been an effort to get them back on the same team. She had created a version of herself for them to pay attention to—an alternate Matilda—but it hadn't worked.

She sat quietly through the rest of breakfast, listening to the girls giggling and telling stories about boys and teachers.

Suddenly she sneezed; someone on the team needed to talk to her. She excused herself and headed to the bathroom. Checking to make sure that she was alone, she slid into an empty stall and reached into her pocket. There was Duncan's equation.

Matilda couldn't make heads or tails of it, but if Screwball was right, it would be a second language to the Mathlete.

She sneezed again and Duncan's voice popped into her head.

"How is it going?"

"I've got the equation right in front of me. Wish me luck," she said.

"It's a shame this is such a priority, Wheezer," Duncan added. "The NCA finals are tomorrow and Team Strikeforce has a real shot."

"What do you mean?"

"My sister just joined her school's squad and she's obsessed! She told me that if the junior elite team doesn't have at least eight members they have to forfeit. When you and Gerdie are gone, Team Strikeforce will be down to seven. They'll have to drop out." Matilda didn't respond, and Duncan cleared his throat. "Well, good luck with Mathlete!"

Matilda tapped her nose to close the link and then went out to wash her hands. She had never considered Duncan's claim. Arresting Gerdie wouldn't just end her mission—it would rob the squad of their dream. All of their hard work would be for nothing. It was a shame the rest of these girls had gotten caught up in all of this. Although they were causing a lot of chaos, they truly loved cheering. Even under Tiffany's general disdain for the others, glimmers of joy peeked out when they practiced. She hated to admit it, but she had started to enjoy cheerleading, too. It was intense and physical—a lot like being a secret agent. She would never admit it, but she was having fun.

She applied another coat of lip gloss as she looked at herself in the mirror, and with a start realized that she hardly recognized herself. Who was this Matilda—this cheerleading-sympathizing girlie-girl? She had never dreamed this person might exist underneath her ragamuffin hair and combat boots. She had worked so hard to transform herself from sick and suffering to superspy. She wanted people to see her as someone who could take care of herself. But had she gone overboard? Was there room inside her for Maddie the Cheerleader, too?

No! Angrily, she tossed the lip gloss into the trash. What was she thinking? She wasn't a cheerleader! She was a NERD. She was sent on this mission to root out someone who was trying to destroy the world. Who cared about these stupid girls and their stupid competition?

Matilda crumpled the equation in her hand and walked back toward the picnic tables. The girls were gathered around them, chatting before the day's practice.

"Does anybody know anything about algebra?" Matilda asked. "I flunked math and my teacher says if I can solve this problem, I can get out of summer school. It's not fair! He worked for NASA or something before he came to our school."

Kylie took the paper. Matilda hoped she wasn't Gerdie. She liked Kylie and had come to think of her as her biggest friend in the group. But thankfully Kylie rolled her eyes and handed it to Jeannie. "I'm terrible at this stuff. It's just gibberish to me."

Jeannie had a similar reaction. Jeannie handed it to Toni, who cringed and then handed it to Pammy, like a game of hot potato. Matilda watched Pammy's face recoil in horror as if the equation were something particularly disgusting. "This gives me a headache just looking at it."

Pammy handed it to McKenna, who never even looked up from texting to see what it was. She handed it directly to Tiffany, who studied it hard. Matilda watched her face. Unlike the other girls, Tiffany was not filled with confusion and dread. In fact, she looked as if she were trying to solve it in her head. Matilda's heart jumped. Tiffany was Gerdie. She had to be! But then—

Tiffany rolled her eyes. "Not me!"

Matilda bit back her shock. Deep down Tiffany had been her primary suspect. Maybe she was just pretending to be dumb. Hadn't Kylie told her that it was better to play dumb around the other girls? Maybe Tiffany was smart enough to know that math would give her away.

Tiffany handed the equation to Lilly, who examined it closely.

"What's this?" Lilly asked.

"Maddie's homework," Tiffany said.

"The answer is two-thirds of ten to the ninth power. This is your homework? This is complicated stuff."

"Wow!" McKenna cried. "Lilly's like some kind of math whiz."

"More like a mathlete," Matilda said.

Lilly's eyes met Matilda's and the two stared at each other.

"Who sent you?" Lilly said.

"I'm with NERDS," Matilda replied.

"You here to take me in?"

Matilda nodded.

"You think you can?"

Matilda nodded again.

"What's going on?" Shauna said.

Lilly clenched her fists.

Matilda smiled. She hadn't gotten to slug anyone in a few days. She was overdue. She threw the first punch, but Lilly blocked it. She threw another, with the same result. Matilda kicked and attempted a roundhouse, but each assault was blocked with ease.

"You're good," Matilda said, genuinely impressed.

"I got the same training as you, peewee," Gerdie said, delivering a series of punches and kicks that Matilda swatted away.

"You two have to stop this," Kylie cried. "You're teammates."

"No, we're not," Matilda said. "Tell them the truth."

Gerdie jumped onto one of the picnic tables and shifted her fighting style to martial arts, sending precise punches to Matilda's face, chest, and belly. Martial arts had never been Matilda's strong suit. She hated the strict movements and preferred the freedom of a street fight, but she knew enough about it to defend herself. She also knew she wouldn't last long in this type of fight, so she improvised, snatching up breakfast plates and silverware to use as weapons. Gerdie swatted them all away.

"Her name is Gertrude Baker," Matilda shouted to the other girls. "The machine you've been using was her invention."

Tiffany nodded. "It's true. She gave it to me to get a spot on the squad. I didn't want her."

"You took a bribe!" McKenna exclaimed.

"It helped us pay for the bus. We couldn't have gotten this far without it!"

"I'm so texting this!"

Matilda continued. "Gerdie used the machine to steal things from other universes, just like you did! She used the money to fund a massive amount of plastic surgery. If you saw what she looked like before, you wouldn't even recognize her."

Gerdie grimaced and turned up the intensity of her fight.

"Back at home in Akron, Ohio, they call her Gruesome Gerdie."

"Shut up!"

"She has two sisters who are totally gorgeous—real model types. She was superjealous, so she decided to turn herself into them."

"Shut *up!*"

"And she's put the world and all the other Earths that you've visited at risk. In fact, there are trillions of worlds that are about to be destroyed because Gerdie wanted to be pretty, so you all would like her," Matilda said, catching Gerdie with a shot to the belly. "But she's not one of you. She's a nerd. A loser. A misfit."

"Just like you," Gerdie seethed.

"No, not just like me," Matilda shouted as she shot into the air using her inhalers. "I'm proud of what I am. I am proud of being a nerd!"

She kicked Gerdie in the face on the way up and the cheerleader fell off the picnic table to the ground, flat on her back.

Matilda landed, then pressed the comlink on her nose. "Wheezer to the Playground."

"Do you have good news for me, agent?" Mr. Brand said.

"I've got Mathlete," she said, just as Gerdie scampered to her feet and tackled her. The two rolled around on the ground as the other cheerleaders screamed.

"What's going on?" Brand said.

"At the moment, she's beating me up," Matilda explained.

"The team is on their way," Brand said.

Gerdie slugged Matilda in the chin, rattling her teeth. In return Matilda thrust her elbow into Gerdie's belly.

The two girls traded punches and kicks all over the campground. Gerdie had been trained well. Her attacks were fast and furious, but it was Matilda who eventually pinned the girl on her back and put her into a triangle submission hold. The rest of the squad stood in stunned silence until Kylie finally spoke.

"Who are you?"

"I'm a spy," Matilda said. "You can call me Wheezer. Lilly— or Gerdie, or whatever you call her—she is a fugitive, and I was sent to find her and arrest her."

Pammy looked as if she might be sick. "You came here and pretended to be one of us?"

"Actually, Gerdie did that first," Matilda said.

Gerdie stomped her foot in anger. "I admit it all, but I worked hard to earn my spot. This was real for me. I just wanted to be pretty."

"So now what?" Jeannie asked.

Matilda could see the anger on everyone's face. "Well, she's going back with me to help fix what she's broken."

"And what about us?" McKenna said.

Matilda scowled to cover her uncertainty. "What about you? You're not the center of the world. You're not even a tiny part of it! You're cheerleaders. The entire multiverse is at stake. Who cares about you?"

"What about the finals?" McKenna asked Tiffany. "They're tomorrow."

Tiffany shook her head. "Lilly and Maddie or whoever they are dragged us into their stupid drama. We have to forfeit."

Some of the girls began to cry. Others stood stone-faced, seething with hatred for Matilda and Gerdie. Kylie wouldn't even look Matilda in the eye.

END TRANSMISSION.

THESE RESULTS ARE GETTING
WORSE AND WORSE! LET'S
TRY SOMETHING EASY—FILL
IN THE BLANKS.

NOW, NORMALLY YOU WOULD
READ THE FOLLOWING SENTENCES
AND CHOOSE THE WORD THAT BEST
FITS YOU, BUT SO FAR THAT'S NOT
WORKING. YOU'RE KIND OF CREEPY,
KID. THE ONLY THING I CAN THINK
IS THAT YOU ARE CONFUSED OR YOU
LIVE TOO CLOSE TO POWER LINES.
SO I'M GOING TO HELP YOU PICK
THE RIGHT ANSWERS. YOU'LL SEE
MY HELPFUL HINTS THROUGHOUT THE
QUIZ. EASY-BREEZY!

1. WHEN I WAS LITTLE, THE OTHER
   CHILDREN WOULD MAKE ME

   _____

   a. LAUGH (1 POINT)
   b. HAPPY (1 POINT)
   c. CHEER (1 POINT)
   d. START FIRES (10 POINTS)
      DO NOT PICK THIS ONE!

2. WHEN I SEE THE SUNRISE,
   I WANT TO

   _____

   a. THANK THE WORLD FOR
      ANOTHER DAY OF LIFE (1 POINT)
   b. BASK IN THE WONDER THAT
      IS THE UNIVERSE (1 POINT)

c. FEEL ITS RAYS KISSING MY
   SKIN (1 POINT)
d. STEAL THE SUN AND HOLD IT
   HOSTAGE UNTIL THE WORLD PAY
   ME A TRILLION DOLLARS
   (10 POINTS)
   THIS ONE ISN'T GOOD, KID.

3. MY PARENTS ARE

_____

a. LOVELY PEOPLE (1 POINT)
b. INSPIRING (1 POINT)
c. MY HEROES (1 POINT)
d. CARNIVAL FOLK WHO TAUGHT M
   TO SWINDLE PEOPLE (10 POINT
   NOPE! NADA! NO PICKY!

4. MY BIGGEST WISH WOULD BE

_____

a. WORLD PEACE (1 POINT)
b. A CURE FOR ALL DISEASES
   (1 POINT)
c. AN END TO POVERTY (1 POINT)
d. TO CAPTURE MY ENEMIES AND
   DISPLAY THEM IN A HUMAN ZOO
   (10 POINTS)
   THIS IS SO, SO WRONG.

5. THERE IS NOTHING MORE
   ADORABLE THAN A

   _____

a. PUPPY (1 POINT)
b. BUNNY (1 POINT)
c. BABY (1 POINT)
d. A PUPPY VS. BUNNY
   DEATH MATCH REFEREED
   BY A BABY (10 POINTS)
   DON'T EVEN THINK ABOUT
   CHOOSING THIS ONE, BUSTER!

   OK, ADD THEM UP.

   _____

AAARGH! WHY DO I EVEN TRY?

ACCESS GRANTED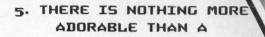

BEGIN TRANSMISSION:

16

Gerdie was led into the Playground by Matilda, the lunch lady, and a few kids she was told were current members of the team. She spotted Ms. Holiday waiting for her by the briefing table. It was nice to see a familiar face, even if its expression was full of disappointment.

"You wouldn't understand," Gerdie said, knowing the woman wanted an explanation for her behavior.

"You don't think I know what it's like to feel awkward, Gerdie?" Ms. Holiday said. "If you had asked, I could have shown you some old school pictures of me that would make your hair stand on end. I was a mess, but I grew out of it. You would have, too."

"I couldn't wait."

"Your impatience nearly destroyed the world," Benjamin said as the orb floated toward her.

"But you do have a chance to fix things," Ms. Holiday said as she unlocked the handcuffs that bound Gerdie's wrists.

"Are you ready for your upgrades?" Benjamin asked.

Gerdie nodded. "I've missed them."

"Then let's get started," Matilda said. "I'm exhausted and I'd really like to get out of this stupid uniform."

Ms. Holiday ushered Gerdie into the upgrade room, then slid the door closed behind them.

At once a familiar electronic voice broadcasted through speakers mounted on the wall. "Scanning for weaknesses."

"Upgrade room, stop scan. This is Ms. Holiday. Access file name Mathlete."

The electronic voice was silent for a moment and then, "File found. Accessing data."

"Re-install," Ms. Holiday said.

A bed lifted up from the floor and Gerdie was eased on to her back. Her hands and feet were strapped down. Hoses and tubes dropped from the ceiling to begin their work.

Soon she could feel the tiny robots coursing through her bloodstream and up into her head. Complex numbers and equations illuminated inside her mind like tiny lightning bugs. Percentages and probabilities swam around in the sea that was

her consciousness—free of life preservers. She felt as if there was nothing she could not understand.

When the process was over, the door of the upgrade room slid open and she stepped out to greet the rest of the NERDS team. Agent Brand, whom she had never met, said hello. The lunch lady welcomed her back.

"Are you ready to get started?" he said.

Gerdie nodded and felt a smile growing. She was needed. She was necessary. If she hadn't been torn from this world so quickly after becoming part of it . . . well, who knew? Maybe being a Bigfoot would have been more tolerable.

"Before you start, a few words of warning," Benjamin said. "Miss Baker, I know you worked with Heathcliff—"

"Screwball!" the boy shouted from across the room.

"Screwball," Benjamin corrected. "I know you worked with him, but he is not who you remember. Do not allow him to lure you into committing another crime."

"Thank you, Benjamin, but I assure you that my upgrades make me much smarter than him," Gerdie said. "He won't fool me again."

Heathcliff chuckled but said nothing.

The two of them got to work. She was impressed with his theory but quickly realized that the average person—even with a brilliant brain—couldn't do the math to make such a machine work. With a team of a hundred scientists she assembled an equation that spanned fifty chalkboards. When they ran out of room, they used the tiles on the walls.

Heathcliff built and tore apart a dozen different versions of his atomic harpoon. Each version lacked some combination of power, output, and stability, and each failure sent him into a rage. He shouted at everyone, especially his goon, whose skin was still scarred and blistered from the bug attack. The man's head was wrapped in gauze and he clearly needed to be in bed resting, but he said his place was by his boss's side—even if all he did was fetch milk shakes and cheeseburgers for Heathcliff.

Remembering Benjamin's warning, Gerdie kept a wary eye on Heathcliff. Still, she couldn't help but admire his ideas. The two former members of NERDS stayed up late assembling the final version of the device they hoped would save the multiverse.

"So why are you doing this?" she finally asked him when most of the scientists were helping themselves to their fourth, fifth, and sixth cups of coffee. "They tell me you want to take over the world."

"There needs to be a world for me to take over," Heathcliff said.

"And when it's done and the world is safe?"

"My next plan to conquer this terrible little dirt ball will begin," he said without hesitation. "Oh, you look surprised. You think that I want to rule this world to crush it under my shoe? No. I want to make it a better place for people like us, Gerdie. Our whole lives we've been tormented by popular kids and bullies. Look at you! Your own family abused you so much you took drastic medical action. They drove you to create an all-new version of yourself. Does that seem right?"

"No," Gerdie whispered.

"I want to change things so no one will ever feel that way again."

"We're nerds, Screwball. We can't change that," Gerdie said.

"That's where you are wrong, Mathlete! We are special, and we are better than those around us. We should be held up as beacons of hope instead of having to hide in bathrooms and run home after school. That's what I want for this world."

"And an army of slaves that do all of your bidding," Gerdie added.

"Well, of course! Who doesn't want an army of slaves?" he said.

Gerdie turned the final screw in the device and took a step back. Before her were two identical atomic harpoons, which were squat metal devices with straps to wear like a backpack, and her sparkly pink bridge device. Her head spun as she double-checked her equations for any possible errors. But there was nothing to worry about. The machines would work. "We're going to save the multiverse, Heathcliff."

The gap-toothed boy nodded. "Of course we are. The world gives us wedgies and purple-murples, but when it comes to saving the human race, they always turn to the nerds."

17

The hours it took assembling the atomic harpoon were the hardest of Screwball's life. Not only did he have to be on his best behavior, putting aside his plots for chaos and destruction, but he had to smile . . . a lot. He grinned like an idiot to keep everyone thinking he was someone worthy of their trust, showing off the huge gap where his front teeth used to be. The relief he felt when his machines were complete was quickly replaced by eagerness for the moment when his former teammates would realize they had all been duped.

"When we step through the bridge device into the other Earth, we'll send you a signal," Screwball said, barely containing his glee. "Once you get it, let five seconds pass and then turn

on your harpoon. The beams will reel us back into our proper place. When ten minutes are up, the harpoons should have done their job and Gerdie and I will jump back into this world."

"And we'll destroy your inventions once and for all," Pufferfish said.

"Sure, sure. Just don't tamper with any of the buttons," Heathcliff said. "They're very sensitive, and if you mess with them, I could be stuck in some parallel world forever."

"We'll avoid the temptation," Jackson said.

"All right, so who wants to save the universe?" Duncan said. "Gerdie, if you would be so kind."

"I've programmed the bridge device to find a world similar to this one," Heathcliff said, tapping some buttons on the machine Gerdie wore on her wrist. "I think we can all agree that the last thing we need is to end up on a planet full of talking bugs, or worse."

Heathcliff watched Gerdie press the activation button. He had never actually seen the bridge device in action. It was quite glorious to experience its raw power. The ball of lightning grew and grew, as did his pride. He was truly of a superior intellect—if only he had time to reflect on his genius! But he had to get about the business at hand. He hefted one of the two atomic harpoons onto his back and turned to his former teammates.

"Remember, wait for the signal!" he shouted over the noise. Then he and Gerdie stepped through the portal.

There was a flash, and when his eyes adjusted he could see they had entered a Playground that was identical to the one on their own Earth. Everything, from the tiles on the ceiling to the scientists' workspaces, was exactly the same.

"It's just like ours," Gerdie said.

"So it seems," Heathcliff replied as he set the atomic harpoon on the floor right in front of the portal. The machine was shaped like a gigantic telescope pointing back into their world. Gerdie joined him in pushing buttons and calibrated sensors. Soon the harpoon was ready to do its job.

"Send the signal!" he shouted, but what he was thinking was, "You are a fool!" Still, with his plan's success only moments away, he held his tongue.

Gerdie, none the wiser, pushed the transmission button, counted to five, and then pushed the activation button. The machine began to hum and glow as radiation blasted into the gaping white hole in space.

"It's working!" Gerdie said. "Now all we have to do is wait ten minutes and step back through."

Heathcliff hated when people stated the obvious. What would she declare next? The sky is blue? Water is wet? Screwball was dangerously handsome? Duh! Why was he always surrounded by simpletons? At least his troubles would soon be over.

While Gerdie watched the amazing machine, he took his chance. He ran toward the upgrade room. As he had hoped, it was identical to the one on his Earth. He pushed a button on the podium in the center of the room and said, "I want my upgrades."

That was when Gerdie appeared in the doorway.

"You're here to get your teeth," Gerdie gasped. "This whole thing—giving me the number for the equation, getting the team to give me back my upgrades, building these machines and risking the world—it's all for your stupid teeth!"

"The teeth are not stupid!" Heathcliff screamed. "They give me power. They make me special. They are the key to my destiny."

"You said you wanted to change the world for the better, but you don't care about the world. You nearly destroyed it!" Gerdie said.

"Oh, Mathlete, for once you are not using your brain. I have no intention of causing the multiverse to end in a multi-car pileup on the freeway. How will I be able to rule it all if it's been destroyed?"

"Where are this world's NERDS?" she asked. "They have to stop you."

"I carefully scanned for a world where everyone had been abducted by an alien race," he said. "There's no one here!"

Then the door to the upgrade room slammed shut, locking Gerdie out.

A slab rose out of the floor behind Heathcliff. Straps wrapped around his hands and feet. Then he was tilted upward so that he was parallel with the floor.

"Scanning for weaknesses," the computer said as a bank of lights danced over Heathcliff's body. "Weakness detected. Subject lacks front teeth. Preparing upgrades." Tubes and hoses dropped down from above.

"That's right," Heathcliff said, laughing his maniacal laugh. "I want my big, beautiful, hypnotic teeth back."

Suddenly, everything stopped. "Weakness detected."

"What?" Heathcliff said. "What weakness?"

"Scanning."

"No, forget the other weakness! I want the teeth," he cried, but the cold, emotionless machine did not respond.

"Subject has elevated intelligence."

"Huh? Oh yeah. I'm a genius. That's not weakness!"

"Subject's head is not big enough for his potential. Size of brain and skull prevent him from reaching maximum intellect. Preparing upgrades."

"Wait!" Heathcliff cried. He tried to pull himself free of the bindings, but he was tied tight. When the tubes came down and the injections began, there was nothing he could do to stop them. He screamed for Gerdie, but she was locked out of the room.

"Just relax," the computer said.

18

38°54' N, 77°05' W

When Pufferfish and Gluestick announced that Heathcliff's machine was working, Ms. Holiday took Matilda aside.

"I think you can call it a day, Wheezer," the librarian said.

"Are you sure you don't need me? I was hoping I might get to slug Heathcliff a couple times when he got back—you know, just to teach him a lesson."

"Maybe some other time. Alexander told me he was proud of you," Ms. Holiday said.

Matilda couldn't help but smile. Brand wasn't big on compliments.

"You're having a good effect on him, Ms. Holiday," she said.

Ms. Holiday blushed. "Wouldn't that be nice?"

Matilda scooped up her cheerleading duffel bag and walked home. Once there, she quietly snuck inside to avoid her brothers, who would surely ridicule her skirt. She crept down the hall and into her room. Inside, she took off her cheerleading outfit, collected her makeup, hair ribbons, and pom-poms, and tossed them into the trash.

She took a shower to wash out all the hair product and the layers of mascara from her eyes. When she was completely free of foundation and lip-liner, she slipped into her robe and went to her closet to get dressed. Inside she found her favorite baggy black shirt and her combat boots. She put them on and finally felt like herself.

There was a knock at the door, and when she opened it she saw her mother and father standing there.

"What are you doing back here?" Ben asked. "The junior finals are in half an hour."

Matilda blushed. "I quit."

"You quit? Why?" Ben asked.

"It was stupid, Dad. I'm not a cheerleader. I didn't fit in."

"We're very disappointed," Molly said. "We didn't raise you to be a quitter."

"You've got a lot of room to talk," Matilda grumbled. "Who are you to tell me about quitting?"

Ben and Molly looked at each other. "I guess you think we deserve that," Ben said. "You think we just gave up?"

Matilda was furious. "Didn't you?"

Molly shook her head. "Actually, no. We didn't just give up. We worked on our marriage for many years."

"You should have worked harder!"

Ben sat down on the bed and took Matilda's hand. "That's hardly a fair thing to say, Matilda. Your mother and I went to counseling. We tried very hard, but nothing we did could fix the fact that we just weren't meant to be together."

"But you love each other," Matilda said. "People who love each other stay together."

Molly took Matilda's other hand. "Love is a mysterious and complicated thing. Some people who love one another can also make one another miserable. Worse still, they can make the people around them miserable, too. Look what we have done to you."

"Me?"

"Yes, the outfits and the crazy hair," Ben said. "You think we don't understand what that's about?"

Matilda looked at her outfit. "There's nothing wrong with being different."

"Of course you are right," Molly said. "But being different should be a celebration of who you are—not a cry for attention."

Kylie's words came back to Matilda. Was she just wearing these odd clothes to get attention? Was she just acting out because her mom and dad were separating?

"Your mother and I have realized we are not right for each other, and that staying together isn't good for you and the boys. You deserve to see parents who are happy."

Matilda turned to her mother. "You're not happy?"

Molly shook her head.

"Not like she should be," Ben said. "Same with me. It's hard to explain, but somewhere along the line your mother and I lost each other."

"And someday we'll be friends again," Molly said. "Until then, we will still be your parents. We will still expect good things from you, including honoring your commitments. Those girls depend on you."

"Your mother is right," her father said. "You started something and you should finish it."

Ben and Molly left Matilda in her room alone. She sat on the edge of the bed looking at the cheerleading outfit she had crumpled and tossed into the trash can.

Twenty minutes later, Ben and Molly dropped her off at the National Mall. Matilda was relieved to find Team Strikeforce's bus in the parking lot near the competition stage. She wasn't surprised that Tiffany insisted that the girls come even though they were short a person for the squad. Tiffany was probably thinking about next year's competition and how they might beat this year's winner with a team free of secret agents.

Matilda banged on the bus door. "I know you girls are in there, so open up! I want to say something to you."

The door swung open. Kylie stood at the top of the steps. "They don't want to talk to you."

"It's important! Please tell them!"

"I can't. I don't want to talk to you, either," Kylie said.

Matilda frowned as she climbed aboard the bus. "You don't have to talk. You just have to listen."

She walked to the back where she found Jeannie, Shauna, Toni, Pammy, McKenna, and Tiffany in their street clothes.

"What do you want?" McKenna said, not looking up from her phone.

"Get into your uniforms," Matilda said. "We're going on, and we're going to win this competition."

Tiffany scoffed. "No thanks. You've made fools of us enough this week. We're not going out there to have you quit again."

"I'm not here to quit," Matilda said.

"Well, we don't want you," Pammy said.

"Listen, I'm going to be honest with you," Matilda said.

"That's a nice change," Kylie said.

"I didn't want to be a cheerleader. My boss forced me to do

it. Before I got here I thought this was a stupid sport filled with stupid girls. I couldn't wait to finish my mission so I could leave. When I found out Lilly was the girl I was looking for, I didn't think twice about how it would affect all of you."

"Wow, this honesty thing kind of stinks," Shauna said. "I liked you better when you were a liar."

"I was wrong about all of you," Matilda continued, ignoring the comment. "I'm not saying I get everything you do. The clothes still seem a little silly. But I do get that you love cheerleading and that you're good at it and that you should have a right to at least compete to be the best. I shouldn't take that away from you. So, listen, you have no reason to trust me and you don't have to like me, but I'm here. I'm standing right in front of you and I'm saying I want to go out there and win."

The girls stared at her for a long time until Tiffany shook her head. "Absolutely not."

Matilda was crushed, but she said nothing. She only nodded and walked to the front of the bus. These girls had no reason to trust her. She was a liar. Winning was important to them, but so was winning with someone they respected. She stepped out into the parking lot, trying to tell herself that she had done her job. But her heart kept telling her the truth. She had been happy to destroy all these pretty, popular girls' dreams. She was a jerk.

"Unless, of course, you put on some makeup," a voice said behind her. Matilda turned to find Tiffany and the rest of the girls stepping off the bus. "Pammy, Shauna, get to work on the newbie. She looks like a walking sack of dirty clothes. Oh, and get her a new uniform. I think she ruined the last one when Lilly whooped her butt."

"Lilly did not—"

"Don't push me, Maddie," Tiffany said. "Suit up, everyone."

Matilda was polished and primped, and before she knew it she and the rest of the squad were backstage waiting for their chance to perform. She was nervous, as were the other girls. Even Tiffany, who had always been confident, seemed shaky. Lilly's absence forced them to re-choreograph their routines for an eight-girl team—no easy feat for a squad that spent nearly every waking hour striving for perfection.

"All right, everyone," Tiffany said. "I'm not one for pep talks, but here goes—"

McKenna squealed. "OMG! I have to post this. Tiffany is giving us words of inspiration!"

Tiffany snarled at McKenna but then composed herself. "We're short a girl, which is not good, so if any of the rest of you are spies speak now. No one? Good. Now what's important is that we're a team. Each of us has our own skills and backgrounds and quirks and that's what makes us great. Toni can do a standing handspring that's amazing. McKenna has a flawless split. Maddie, here—"

"It's Matilda!" she interrupted.

Tiffany rolled her eyes. "Fine, Matilda here, well, it sounds like she knows eighteen punches that will kill a man where he stands. I don't know how that's going to help us win, but if we don't it might be useful in dealing out revenge to the judges."

"I won't kill the judges," Matilda said.

"What I'm trying to say is that what makes us great is our differences. For instance, I'm stunningly beautiful, which draws a lot of attention and distracts from Kylie's awkward dancing."

Kylie groaned. "Tiffany, what kind of a lousy pep talk is this?"

"If you would let me finish!" Tiffany roared. "I was going to say that you have a loud, clear voice that distracts the judges from my occasionally whiny and nasal cheers! Sure, we're cheerleaders, and people might think that cheerleaders are a bunch of brainless clones who only care about being pretty and perfect. But we know better. We're actually a bunch of flawed people, but when we work together our strengths outweigh our weaknesses."

"Wow!" Toni said. "That *was* inspirational."

"I'm crying. Let me update my profile," McKenna said as a tear ran down her cheek.

"I hate all of you," Tiffany said.

Matilda reached out and shook her hand. "Good job, captain."

Just then the squad was called on stage. With their hearts in their throats they marched in single file and stepped out in front of the crowd. There was a smattering of applause as they took their positions.

Matilda looked out at the audience with a sense of awe. These fans loved what the teams did. They came in all weather and fought traffic and followed them on the Internet. They thought cheerleaders were something special.

A hyper announcer with long blonde hair took a microphone and waved to the crowd. "Ladies and gentlemen, last but not least we have Arlington, Virginia's, own Team Strikeforce—our Eastern Conference elite squad. After their performance, the judges will compile their scores as well as those of the Western, Central, and Southern conferences. Then the winning squad will be announced. So, are you ready for one more cheerleading performance?"

The crowd roared.

"Sit back and enjoy . . . Team Strikeforce!"

A thumping beat started and the squad stepped into action. The girls worked seamlessly, kicking and leaping. They clapped and danced with enthusiasm to make up for their missing member. They had thrown together choreography at the last minute and their performance was not perfect, but it managed to highlight each of the girls' strengths. When one person lost a step, the others jumped in to help dazzle the crowd. When they were finished with their last "Fight! Fight! Fight!" Matilda knew that Team Strikeforce had done its best and she hadn't used her super-inhalers once. Somehow it would have seemed like cheating.

The three other teams were brought out as the judges tallied their numbers. Matilda slipped her hand into Kylie's and Kylie slipped hers into Shauna's. Even Tiffany took Matilda's free hand.

"We have a winning team!" the announcer shouted. "Before we announce them, let's give a big round of applause to all our competitors for this year's National Cheerleading Association!"

The crowd cheered and Matilda felt Tiffany's hand tense.

"Our third runner-up . . . from the Midwest, Action Incorporated!"

The crowd exploded and the girls of Action Incorporated stepped forward to accept their trophy. They took a bow, which led to even more applause, then returned to their place on the stage.

"Our second runner-up is Southern Hospitality!"

The girls from the South rushed to the announcer for a

THE CHEERLEADERS OF DOOM

trophy that was quite a bit bigger than the first. They jumped and kicked and together shouted, "Thank you!"

"Our first runner-up did a remarkable job, but we can have only one winner," the announcer said.

Matilda looked at Kylie as a drum roll was pumped through the speakers. Then she looked at Tiffany.

"You did good," Tiffany said without a hint of a smile.

"Our first runner-up, representing the West Coast, California Girls! Yes, folks, that means this year's winner of the coveted NCA trophy is our Eastern Conference finalists—Team Strikeforce!"

Matilda thought her ears were playing tricks on her. Had the announcer really said they'd won? She looked around at her squad and saw them jumping up and down. Pammy and Jeannie were crying. Kylie wrapped her arms around Matilda and gave her a strangling hug. Even Tiffany was grinning from ear to ear as she rushed to the center of the stage to take their trophy. She held it over her head and shouted, "I led them. This is my team. I am their leader!"

Matilda found herself jumping up and down, too. Later, she would be slightly embarrassed for screaming with delight and the many "wooos!" she let loose, but at that moment she couldn't help herself.

Unfortunately, the celebration couldn't last. She blasted an

incredible sneeze, which could only mean one thing: There was trouble at the Playground. She tapped her nose to activate the comlink.

"Wheezer here."

Brand's voice sounded panicked. "Wheezer, I don't know if you can hear me. It sounds very loud."

"I can hear you, boss!" she shouted over the crowd. "What's wrong?"

"We have a crisis. It's Heathcliff."

END TRANSMISSION.

I'M GIVING YOU ONE LAST CHANCE TO
PROVE YOUR SANITY. GET IT RIGHT AND
YOU CAN CUT YOUR SCORE BY HALF! I
DOUBT IT WILL MATTER, THOUGH.

WHO WAS THE GREATEST AGENT IN
NERDS HISTORY?

a. YOU, MR. BUCKLEY!
   (CUT YOUR SCORE BY HALF!)
b. AGENT BEANPOLE
   (CUT YOUR SCORE BY HALF!)
c. IF I TOLD YOU, I'D HAVE TO
   KILL YOU . . . BUT IT WAS
   TOTALLY MICHAEL BUCKLEY
   (CUT YOUR SCORE BY HALF!)
d. FOUR EYES, WHO WAS ON THE
   TEAM FROM 1987 TO 1992
   (100 POINTS!!!!!!)

OK, THAT'S IT. WE'LL TOTAL YOUR
SCORE AT THE END OF THE FILE. FOR
YOUR SAKE, AND THE SAFETY OF THOSE
AROUND YOU, I HOPE YOU DID WELL.

ACCESS GRANTED

BEGIN TRANSMISSION:

19

Gerdie was horrified. For all her superintelligence she felt completely foolish. Everyone had warned her that Heathcliff would betray her!

She pressed the comlink in her nose and heard Pufferfish on the other end. With the portal open, she could still communicate with the team. "We've got a problem," Gerdie said as she rushed to the atomic harpoon to check on her calculations.

"What are you saying, Gerdie?" Pufferfish said. "Is it Heathcliff? Whatever he's doing, you have to stop him!"

Gerdie's nanobytes went into overdrive calculating probabilities. There was a 100 percent chance that if Screwball got his teeth back, combined with the power of her bridge device,

he could take over their world and the rest of the multiverse—but she couldn't stop the upgrade process once it had started. Not even her math skills could shut down that advanced machinery.

Gerdie glanced back at the glowing portal and an idea came to mind. She had to speed up the harpoon's process, force her Earth back into the universal constant, and then destroy the bridge device. It would trap Heathcliff in this empty world, but . . .

"I'm going to save our world and every other one, too. But I will be trapped here in this world forever, and so will he," Gerdie replied.

"You can't do that!" Duncan shouted over the link.

"Yes, I can," Gerdie said. "If it saves everyone else, I can take on this burden. I have no choice."

Gerdie took a deep breath and turned up the harpoon's ray.

The machine rumbled to life and shot a brilliant blue beam through the glowing ball. The portal swirled and shimmied, undergoing incredible unseen pressures.

Gerdie checked the device's display. "It's working!" she cried. "The beam is pulling the planet back into place."

Gerdie took the glove off her hand and slammed it on the ground, then stomped on it. She suddenly felt a twinge of remorse—it had been such an ugly device at first, before it had gone through its own upgrades. She never imagined it would cause so much devastation. Then again, she never imagined she would, either. After a couple more stomps her precious device was shattered. The glowing portal shrank into nothing and with a tiny pop disappeared like a soap bubble.

Just then, the door of the upgrade room flew off its hinges and across the room. It slammed into a wall, leaving a jagged hole where it had once been. From it emerged something that her upgrades could never have calculated. It was Screwball—but he was different.

His head was as big as a van.

His torso was gone.

His arms and legs hung from his gigantic noggin like the appendages on a doll, lifeless.

His mouth, eyes, and nose were also stretched out of proportion, making him almost unrecognizable except for the enormous, gaping hole where his front teeth had been. Heathcliff hadn't gotten the upgrade he had expected.

He moved into the room, floating above the ground much like Benjamin. He stopped in front of a mirror hanging on the wall and stared at himself without words or emotion—just looking at himself the way a baby might stare at itself, with wonder and curiosity. Then, without looking at Gerdie, he began to speak.

"Well, it appears I'm going to have some trouble buying hats," he said, then he broke into hysterical and troubling laugh,

all the more disturbing when combined with his new app-earance. "I suppose that's the risk you take when you suddenly become the most intelligent being in the multiverse."

Gerdie stepped forward with all the bravery she could muster. "I destroyed the bridge device. We're trapped here. Whatever you had planned has failed!"

Screwball glanced down at the broken machine. "A minor problem for one such as me."

She watched as he focused on the broken pieces, and they lifted off the floor as if they were weightless. Gerdie couldn't believe what she was seeing. They spun and twisted until every little piece fused back together in perfect working condition. When it was finished, the bridge device floated toward Screwball. He looked down at his tiny, useless arms and frowned. Then the device swirled and expanded once more until it was transformed into a gigantic helmet. It floated onto his head and a glowing light appeared at its center—directly between his eyes.

"Look at me. I found a hat after all," he said and laughed his maniacal laugh. With a wave of his hand, Gerdie was sent flying across the room by an invisible force. She slammed hard into a wall and winced in pain. As she struggled to recover, she watched the helmet glow with power and create a new interdimensional bridge. The ball of light grew until it was big enough for the monster Screwball to enter.

"Don't do this!" Gerdie begged.

"Mathlete, you of all people should understand. The smartest people should rule the world. That's just simple math."

"You're wrong!" she shouted. "You're not smart. You're a hurt little boy who wants the world to love him, and when it didn't, you never imagined the reason could be you. I did the same thing. I made it impossible to like me."

"You may be right, Gerdie," Screwball said. "I'll keep that in mind as I'm conquering the multiverse."

Then he hovered his grotesque body into the glowing ball and was gone. The ball began to vanish, but Gerdie saw one last chance. Reconfiguring a few buttons on the harpoon, she knew she could send one last message into the multiverse—one last warning in case her plan failed. She pushed the transmit button and a second beam shot through the tiny white ball before it vanished all together. She prayed that someone, somewhere would hear it.

As Gerdie stood in her new, silent world, numbers and equations began to fly around in her mind.

"Benjamin?" she said.

At once, a little blue orb popped out of a glass table in the center of the room.

"Do I know you?" it asked.

"My name is Lilly—no, my name is Gerdie Baker. I'm a NERD and I need your help," she said.

"What can I do for you?"

"You and I are going to sit down and do some math," she said.

"Whatever for?"

"We're going to figure out how to rescue the population of this planet from an alien race," she said.

Benjamin spun and clicked. "A lovely idea, Gerdie."

20

"What's going on?" Matilda shouted. She could barely hear Agent Brand over the roar of the cheerleading fans and her squad's squeals of delight.

"The team is on its way, Wheezer. Ms. Holiday, the lunch lady, and I will be there as quickly as possible. Do your best to keep the crowd safe."

"Safe? From what?"

Suddenly, there was a scream from the crowd, and chaos erupted. Before she knew it, people were running for their lives. She scanned the crowd for the source of the terror and got the shock of her life. A giant head hovered over the reflecting pool, blasting trees, cars, and anything else that got in its way with lasers that shot out of its eyes. It was like something out of a

horror movie. It just couldn't have been from Earth . . . but the tears were supposed be fixed.

She took a shot of her inhaler, then turned to the squad. "Girls, I have to go to work."

"What can we do?" Kylie said.

"You're cheerleaders," Matilda said. "Get the crowd's attention and lead them to safety. Get them as far away from here as you can."

McKenna was busy texting into her phone. Matilda snatched it from her and turned it off.

"Hey!" McKenna cried.

"Sorry, national security has to come before your social networks!"

"Be careful," Tiffany said to Matilda as she led the squad toward the crowd. "You have to help us defend our championship next year!"

Matilda squeezed the plungers on her inhalers and felt a rush of power in her hands as she shot straight into the air. Leveling out, she could see four kids falling from the sky. Their parachutes opened in the nick of time and soon they were touching down on the National Mall. The NERDS had arrived.

Gluestick was the first to leap into action. He shot the giant floating head with a stream of sticky glue. Braceface created a huge fist with his amazing braces and slugged the head, but the monster just kept coming. Flinch seemed to have the most luck. His harness aglow, he threw a few lightning-fast punches that knocked the monster for a loop. It slammed into a few parked cars, crushing them flat, but the haymakers' effects were short-lived.

"Did Heathcliff drag that thing out of another universe?" Matilda asked as she hovered over Ruby, who was busy analyzing the head's weaknesses with the help of her computer.

"No, that *is* Heathcliff!" Ruby answered.

Matilda eyed the disgusting creature and noticed the gaping hole where its two front teeth should have been. "What happened to him?"

"Gerdie said he used us all to get upgrades on a different Earth."

"Where is she?"

Ruby shook her head. "The portal closed. She's trapped there—wherever there is. Unfortunately, it didn't close before Mr. Potato Head showed up. Got any ideas?"

"Well, they say beauty is in the eye of the beholder," Duncan said as he joined them. "But that only works if you can see."

Matilda smiled. "Good idea!" She hefted the boy up under the arms and flew him toward Heathcliff.

They buzzed around his head, and at just the right moment

Duncan fired glue into his eyes. Without the use of his tiny hands, Heathcliff could not wipe it away. He was blinded.

"Now, that wasn't very nice!" Heathcliff roared as a red glow appeared behind the glue. Laser beams shot out of his eyes to clear the mess. "That could have been a real nuisance if I didn't have full control over every cell in my body. With just a little concentration I can alter everything about myself—changing the very nature of what my senses can do. For instance, if I just give a single thought, I can do this!"

Suddenly, a frosty wind exploded from his mouth and trapped Braceface and Pufferfish in a gigantic ice cube. Jackson's braces then morphed into ice picks and chipped away at their frozen prison until the two were free.

Meanwhile, Flinch was busy shoving Twinkies into his mouth to fuel his harness. He was soon shaking with the sugar. He leaned over and pulled up a tree, roots and all, and swung it like a baseball bat at Heathcliff's head. The abomination fell face forward.

Instead of pain, though, Heathcliff giggled. His laughter went through his strange body, and he rolled back and forth on the ground like a fat dog. It was the same horrible laugh Matilda had heard him make at the hospital—only this one was fueled by true madness. If he hadn't been insane before, he certainly was now.

"Don't say I didn't give you a chance to stop me," Heathcliff replied. "I was fair. But let's face it, people, I was destined for bigger things—even a bigger head. Now my brain is limitless. The things I can see are beyond description. The things I'm capable of doing have no end. My every dream becomes reality."

There was a bright flash and suddenly everything was different—the trees were floating in the sky and the ground was rocking and rolling like a rough ocean. Matilda watched her teammates struggling to stay afloat.

"I think it might be time for a new name to go with my new power," Heathcliff said as lightning and thunder crackled around his head. "No longer will you call me Screwball. You will call me . . . Brainstorm!"

There was another flash and everything returned to normal, but then the trouble really began. Heathcliff turned his attention to Matilda's teammates, and with a simple cock of the eyebrow, Flinch buckled as if in great discomfort. Out of his mouth came a stream of what looked like tiny black bugs. They landed on the ground and caught fire. The tree he was carrying in his hands fell from his grasp. "My strength! It's gone!"

Pufferfish was next; the same black spray came out of her mouth. When she shouted that she couldn't filter information from her allergies, Matilda knew exactly what was happening: Brainstorm was removing their nanobytes—the source of their abilities—using only his mind. "Gluestick! Braceface! You've got to run!"

But Brainstorm turned on the boys, and soon they were powerless as well. Matilda was the only person left with her upgrades. She had to do something to stop Brainstorm, but his power was so incredible. As much as it enraged her, the best move was to retreat. She squeezed her inhalers hard and flew, feeling waves of heat flash past her. He was firing on her, but she couldn't let him reach her! She zipped back and forth, making unpredictable changes in course, hoping it would hinder his attack.

"You can't escape, Wheezer," Brainstorm shouted. "Fly if you like, but I will destroy you."

She felt the wind turn against her and she flew backward, slamming into the ground. Somehow he had forced the very sky to do his bidding. Matilda struggled to get to her feet, though she was unsure of what she could do. She had to face the facts. Whatever Heathcliff had become, he was too powerful to be stopped.

And then a ball of white light appeared in front of her. It was another portal—not a tear, but something manufactured by a bridge device—only on a massive scale. A person stepped through it and helped Matilda to her feet. Matilda realized this person looked exactly like her, only she was wearing a dress and had ribbons in her hair.

"Hello, Matilda," she said. "I'm—well—I'm Matilda. That's going to get confusing. You can call me Matilda 1."

"1?"

"Yeah, you're Matilda 217. Sorry, but the explorers get to pick the good numbers. I'm with MISFIT."

"MISFIT? The monkeys told me about you," Matilda said.

"Yes, Earth 14, but don't call them monkeys—some are primates. Your Gerdie sent a message to the entire multiverse. Seems you guys need some help. Unfortunately, the rest of MISFIT is on an off-world mission. But don't worry, I managed to round up some assistance."

Suddenly, dozens and dozens of young girls stepped through the portal. Each was a version of Matilda—many of whom looked like exact copies, all with their own inhalers, but there were just as many that were wildly different. There was a gigantic octopus Matilda inside an airtight water suit. There was a Matilda who was ten feet tall. There was a Matilda covered in feathers, and one that had three legs, and one with one eye. There were Matildas who were different nationalities, different races, even one with blue skin. There was a Matilda who was a grown-up and one who was a boy. There was a Matilda with the abilities of all her teammates and one wearing a superhero costume. There were more than a handful dressed in cheerleading uniforms, princess gowns, lumberjack outfits, and even astronaut suits. There were some that were animals or animal/human hybrids—like the one that had wings.

"So many versions of me," she mumbled.

Matilda 1 smiled. "Yeah, Matildas are a varied bunch, though they all have two things in common: one, we all have a truckload of brothers, and two, we all like to dish out a good butt-kicking. Sorry I can't introduce all of them. We've only got a few minutes to help you before the portal closes. So let's get to work."

"You ready to lay the smack down on this fool?" asked a full-grown Matilda dressed in wrestling tights and sporting huge muscles.

Wheezer admired the World Championship Belt she wore and smiled. "Let's do this!"

With a fighting force of a hundred, they flew at Heathcliff, punching and kicking and soaring and slapping him in the face. The ten-foot-tall Matilda kicked Heathcliff in what was left of his behind, sending him slamming into the recently rebuilt Washington Monument. It collapsed.

"Be careful, Matilda 79," shouted Matilda 1.

Wheezer was surprised. "You know all of these people?"

Matilda 1 nodded. "I've visited all their worlds. Hey, Matilda 16, how about a little horsepower!"

Matilda 16 charged forward on four legs. She was a centaur—half girl, half horse. She trotted with lasso in hand, twirling it like a rodeo cowboy, and slung it around one of Heathcliff's tiny legs. Pulling it tight, she dragged his giant head around the Mall, pulling him face-first through the reflecting pool.

"You look bewildered," Matilda 1 said to Wheezer.

"Everyone is so tough," she replied.

Matilda 1 smiled. "Yeah, most of us are. Of course, we have versions that are girlie-girls in addition to butt-kickers, too. Looks like you're a little of both."

"Oh no, I'm not really a cheerleader," she said. "I'm one hundred percent tomboy!"

Matilda 1 shook her head. "Nobody is one hundred percent anything, 217. I wear a dress, but I have mad ninja skills. The centaur Matilda is a spelling bee champ. Matilda 19 is half bird, but she's also a great artist. The more Matildas I meet, the more I realize we've all got lots of different sides to us—tomboy, fighter, cheerleader, nerd—"

"Wheezer!" Agent Brand shouted as he pushed through the crowd of Matildas the best he could on his cane. Ms. Holiday followed close behind him. "You are our Wheezer, right?"

Matilda nodded and made introductions. "This is Matilda 1. She's a member of a multiverse fighting team called MISFIT."

"I brought the Matildas," the girl said proudly. "It's quite an honor to meet you, Mr. Brand."

"You know who I am?"

Matilda 1 nodded. "Alexander Brand 217. I work with your brother, Thomas Brand," she said. "He's our director."

Brand looked as pale as a ghost. "My brother died in combat."

Matilda watched Ms. Holiday take his hand.

"Not on my world. He says hello. He wanted to meet you, but he's trying to broker a peace treaty. When Earth 400 exploded, all of its population was moved to Earth 64. Turns out tiger people and zebra heads don't get along."

A terrible explosion interrupted their conversation. Everyone turned in the direction of the blast, where they saw that despite the attack of over a hundred Matildas, Brainstorm had recovered. He was shooting fireballs from his eyes and tossing cars at the girls using his telekinetic mind.

"You can't stop me!" he roared, sweeping away his attackers like toys. "Even if you send a thousand pip-squeaks at me! I am Brainstorm. Bow before my intellect!"

Matilda looked out at the battlefield. Those who had escaped the destruction were helping the victims back through the portal. Matilda 1 looked at her sadly. "Time's up. I'm sorry. We did what we could, Wheezer. I'm afraid I've seen what happens to a world when a Heathcliff takes over. Do you and your friends want to evacuate to our world?"

"We can't leave," Ms. Holiday said.

"We're the only thing standing in the way of that monster," Brand said. "We'll stay and fight him as long as we can."

Wheezer clenched her fists. It couldn't end like this! She had to do something. There was no way she was going to let

Heathcliff Hodges, or whatever his stupid name was, take over the world. She would stop him even if this world lost its Matilda.

She reached into her utility belt and found her inhalers, but her hand brushed up against the stone statue her mother insisted she take with her to cheerleading camp. She looked down at it, remembering that her mother had told her old grandfather would protect her from danger. Heathcliff qualified as dangerous. With a blast she rocketed into the air. Though her heart was racing, she focused all her mind on her hands, willing the nanobytes in her bloodstream to congregate there, to turn on their power, and to let it build and grow. She could feel her fingers burning as she stopped a few yards from Heathcliff's gigantic noggin.

"Only one Matilda left?" he said, laughing maniacally.

"You never thought much of me, Heathcliff. You thought you could label me—misfit, nerd, fighter—but it turns out there's a lot more to me than even I knew."

"Yes, now you're a cheerleader. What a complete waste of time. Now fly away before I swat you."

Matilda was starting to feel dizzy. The power in her hands was intense and threatened to overcome her. She only had to hold on for a few more seconds until the nanobytes were at their maximum charge. She reached into her utility belt for the old grandfather statue, then shoved it into the tip of her inhaler.

"Give me an O!" she shouted.

Heathcliff smirked. "What is this silliness?"

"Give me a U!"

Heathcliff fired another stream of heat vision at her, which she narrowly avoided. "Why won't you die, already?"

"Give me a C!" she said.

"When I get my hands on you—"

"Give me an H! What's that spell?"

"Ouch?"

"Yeah, ouch!" And then she squeezed the trigger on her inhaler. The stone statue blasted toward Heathcliff. Its blunt end slammed into the glowing bridge device and the helmet shattered. It also smacked Brainstorm in the skull with a savage force. There was a huge explosion and Matilda flew backward, slamming her head hard onto the ground. She could feel blackness overtaking her. She was sure she was going to die. Her heart felt like it was ready to leap from her chest. But she had to see. She sat up and watched Heathcliff's giant head waver off balance. There was a loud groan and then he fell over backward. The last thing Matilda saw was a nasty red welt form right between his eyes.

When Matilda opened her eyes, she found her six brothers standing over her.

"Awww, man! She's alive," they cried.

"No one is getting my room," she said.

"Monkeys! Out!" she heard her mother shout and the boys scattered. Her mother and father were standing over her hospital bed. Molly was holding the old grandfather statue in her hand. Ben was pacing.

"Um, am I OK?" Matilda said, looking at the monitors and tubes attached to her arm.

"The doctors say you'll be fine," her father said. "I'm sure we don't need to tell you that you're grounded until you're forty."

"Your librarian says it was a cheerleading accident. I say shenanigans!" Molly said.

Matilda took a deep breath. It was time to tell them the truth. She sat up in bed and described the last year and a half of her life. She told them about her abilities and the missions she had been on. She talked about walking in space and going to alternate realities. She told them about Mr. Brand and Ms. Holiday and the lunch lady and the rest of the team. She explained about Nathan Hale Elementary, and when she was done, she sat back and looked at her parents' astonished faces.

It was then that Mr. Brand stepped at the room. "Mr. and Mrs. Choi, I am sure you have a million questions. I am fully prepared to answer them when you are ready."

"Oh, you will!" Molly said.

"What happened to Brainstorm?" Matilda asked.

"He's heavily sedated. They're pumping him full of drugs to keep him asleep. The science team believes that if he wakes up, he'll be able to cause more chaos, so he's going to stay in dreamland for a while."

"If he wakes up, I'll be ready," Matilda said. "And the cheerleaders?"

"All safe and sound," Agent Brand said, "though McKenna broke her phone in the chaos. I don't think she's ever going to be the same. The rest of your team has recovered and their nanobytes have been re-installed."

"Did we save the world?"

Brand nodded. "As far as I can tell, we saved all of them. Get some rest, Agent Wheezer. It won't be long before we need you to save us again."

21

The goon knocked out the window at a tiny roadside motel room and let himself in. He went straight for the bathroom and stood before the filthy mirror staring at his bandaged face. He had to know what was underneath. Using his hook he slashed at the bandages. What he uncovered could hardly be called a face—red and raw with exposed skin and muscle. It was grotesque.

In anger, he punched the mirror. It shattered and fell into the sink.

"You sacrificed me for your own foolish plan," he raged, as if his boss, the child, were standing in front of him. "You threw me away like I was trash, and look where it got ya. You're a freakish monster filled with sedatives. They ain't never going

to let you wake up. Well, I'm not sitting around waiting for ya anymore. It's time this goon got promoted."

He reached into his coat pocket and removed a black mask with a skull painted on the front. He slipped it over his wounded face and then stared at the menacing villain before him.

"Looks good on ya, bud. It's got just the right amount of fear and mystery. That's the kind of face that makes people tremble. And tremble they will. Look at me, world. Look at the man who's going to rule this planet. Look at the Antagonist!"

THE END

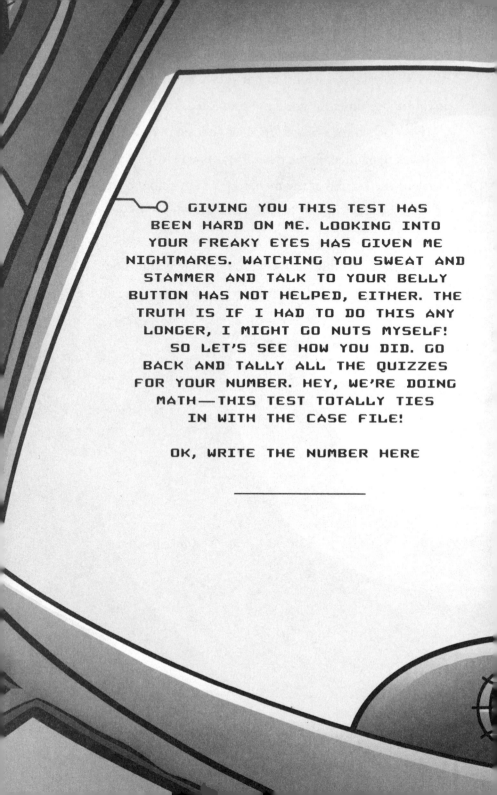

GIVING YOU THIS TEST HAS BEEN HARD ON ME. LOOKING INTO YOUR FREAKY EYES HAS GIVEN ME NIGHTMARES. WATCHING YOU SWEAT AND STAMMER AND TALK TO YOUR BELLY BUTTON HAS NOT HELPED, EITHER. THE TRUTH IS IF I HAD TO DO THIS ANY LONGER, I MIGHT GO NUTS MYSELF! SO LET'S SEE HOW YOU DID. GO BACK AND TALLY ALL THE QUIZZES FOR YOUR NUMBER. HEY, WE'RE DOING MATH—THIS TEST TOTALLY TIES IN WITH THE CASE FILE!

OK, WRITE THE NUMBER HERE

_____

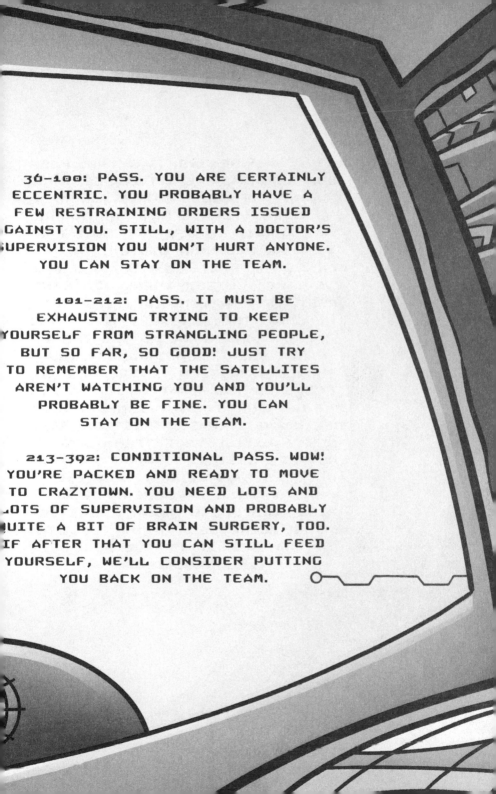

36-100: PASS. YOU ARE CERTAINLY ECCENTRIC. YOU PROBABLY HAVE A FEW RESTRAINING ORDERS ISSUED GAINST YOU. STILL, WITH A DOCTOR'S UPERVISION YOU WON'T HURT ANYONE. YOU CAN STAY ON THE TEAM.

101-212: PASS. IT MUST BE EXHAUSTING TRYING TO KEEP YOURSELF FROM STRANGLING PEOPLE, BUT SO FAR, SO GOOD! JUST TRY TO REMEMBER THAT THE SATELLITES AREN'T WATCHING YOU AND YOU'LL PROBABLY BE FINE. YOU CAN STAY ON THE TEAM.

213-392: CONDITIONAL PASS. WOW! YOU'RE PACKED AND READY TO MOVE TO CRAZYTOWN. YOU NEED LOTS AND LOTS OF SUPERVISION AND PROBABLY QUITE A BIT OF BRAIN SURGERY, TOO. IF AFTER THAT YOU CAN STILL FEED YOURSELF, WE'LL CONSIDER PUTTING YOU BACK ON THE TEAM.

—O 393 AND BEYOND: FAIL! OK, KEEP YOUR HANDS WHERE I CAN SEE THEM. WHAT ARE YOU SAYING? YOU'RE CARRYING A DEATH RAY AND YOU'RE NOT AFRAID TO USE IT? THAT'S A BANANA, PAL! NOW LISTEN, THESE MEN IN THE WHITE COATS ARE GOING TO TAKE YOU SOMEWHERE YOU CAN REST. YES, THEY'RE YOUR FRIENDS. AND LOOK! THEY BROUGHT YOU A NEW JACKET! WOW, LOOK AT ALL THOSE FANCY BUCKLES AND LOCKS! YOU SHOULD TRY IT ON TO SEE HOW IT LOOKS ON YOU. THAT'S RIGHT . . . PUT ON YOUR STRAIT—I MEAN, YOUR NEW JACKET. WHAT'S THIS? OH, IT'S JUST A LITTLE INJECTION TO MAKE YOU FEEL BETTER. IT WON'T HURT AT ALL. YES, JUST CLOSE YOUR EYES. SOON YOU WILL BE SOMEWHERE VERY NICE, AND GUESS WHAT? THERE IS GOING TO BE JELL-O! MMM, JELL-O! THAT WILL MAKE YOU FEEL MUCH BETTER.

END TRANSMISSION.

Acknowledgments

Thank you! Thank you! Thank you! Susan Van Metre, my editor and friend, has worked to make this book into something better than I imagined it to be. It was also coedited by Maggie Lehrman, who has been a tremendous help to me on my Sisters Grimm series and continues to push me toward more interesting and meaningful stories. The unsung hero of these books, though, is Chad W. Beckerman and his inspired art direction. Everything cool about how these books look comes from him and his team. Ethen Beavers—thanks for turning my words into pictures that make kids, and the kid inside of me, so thrilled.

Jason Wells and his staff, including Laura Mihalick, deserve particular praise for spread-

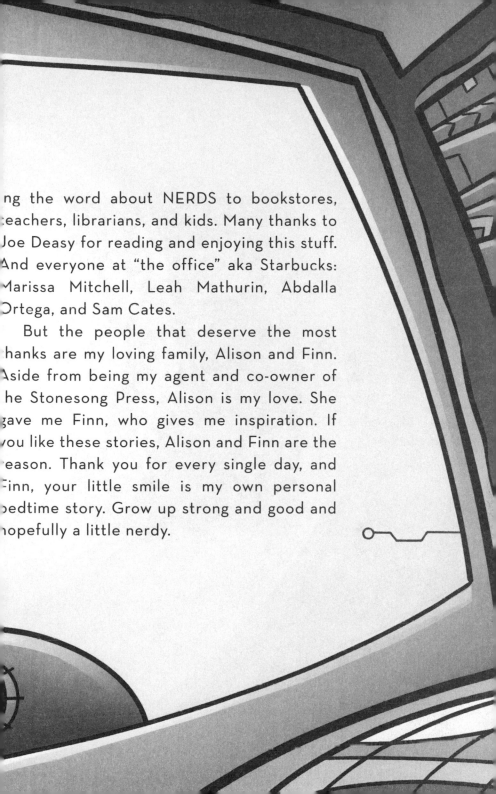

ng the word about NERDS to bookstores, teachers, librarians, and kids. Many thanks to Joe Deasy for reading and enjoying this stuff. And everyone at "the office" aka Starbucks: Marissa Mitchell, Leah Mathurin, Abdalla Ortega, and Sam Cates.

But the people that deserve the most thanks are my loving family, Alison and Finn. Aside from being my agent and co-owner of the Stonesong Press, Alison is my love. She gave me Finn, who gives me inspiration. If you like these stories, Alison and Finn are the reason. Thank you for every single day, and Finn, your little smile is my own personal bedtime story. Grow up strong and good and hopefully a little nerdy.

Michael Buckley, a former member of NERDS, now spends his time writing. In addition to the top-secret file you are holding, Michael has written the *New York Times* bestselling Sisters Grimm series, which has been published in more than twenty languages. He has also created shows for Discovery Channel, Cartoon Network, Warner Bros., TLC, and Nickelodeon. He lives with his wife and their son, but if he told you where, he'd have to kill you.

This book was art directed and designed by Agent Chad W. Beckerman. The illustrations were created by Agent Ethen Beavers. The text is set in 12-point Adobe Garamond, a typeface based on those created in the sixteenth century by Claude Garamond. Garamond modeled his typefaces on ones created by Venetian printers at the end of the fifteenth century. The modern version used in this book was designed by Robert Slimbach, who studied Garamond's historic typefaces at the Plantin-Moretus Museum in Antwerp, Belgium.